AIRBORNE PHOTO

OTHER BOOKS BY CLINT BURNHAM

Be Labour Reading (poetry, ECW Press)

The Jamesonian Unconscious: The Aesthetics of Marxist Theory (Duke University Press)

Fatal femmes: the poetry of Lynn Crosbie (Streetcar Editions)

Airborne Photo

STORIES BY

Clint Burnham

Anvil Press (Vancouver)

Printed and bound in Canada
First Edition
Cover: Rayola Design
Cover photo: Jason Wood

CANADIAN CATALOGUING IN PUBLICATION DATA

Burnham,Clint, 1962-
Airborne photo

ISBN 1-895636-22-1

I. Title
PS8553.U665A77 1999 C813'.54 C99-910329-6
PR9199.3.B79226A7 1999

Represented in Canada by the Literary Press Group
Distributed by General Distribution Services

The publisher gratefully acknowledges the assistance of the B.C. Arts Council and the Canada Council for the Arts.

Anvil Press
Suite 204-A – 175 East Broadway,
Vancouver, BC V5T 1W2 CANADA

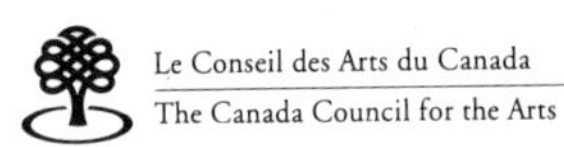

Qui sceptra duro saevus imperio regit,
timet timentes; metus in auctorem redit

The tyrant fears those who fear him;
terror returns to its author's head

—Seneca

Acknowledgments

Some of these stories have appeared in the following magazines & websites: *Paragraph*, *Black Cat 115*, *Urban Graffitti*, *sub-TERRAIN*, *Euphony*, and some other places I've forgotten for legal reasons. I've read them at KSW, UBC, Mike Hansen's studio, Sarah Curry's apartment, the Red Door, Black Sheep Books, The Forbidden Cafe and, again, probably some other places I've forgotten.

Thanks to Julie, Mark, Michael, Judy, Deanna, Karen, Rob, Reid, Kegan, Stephen, Peter, Brian, Dennis, Victor, George, Renee, Kevin, Lillian, Stu, Gil, Michael, Lynn, Fred, Tony, Colin, Simon, Luke, Mo, Lilliam, Gerald, Chantal, Chris, Jeff, Greg, Teresa, Gagun—you guys know why.

Table of Contents

one

two

three

one

«AIRBORNE PHOTO»

I SAT ON A CHAIR facing the pregnant teenager and pointed my gun at her belly. She laughed and said oh no and looked up at me and kissed me. Her hand on my cheek. My girlfriend took the Polaroid. The teenager leaned forward and took a drink.

Remember you're drinking for two, I said.

Earlier I'd walked over with my girlfriend. We'd smoked up so we didn't want to drive. She didn't want to drive her truck. We walked through the leaf-covered streets, and at an intersection a guy in a car laughed at the red stain covering the stomach of my white shirt. I was going to pull my piece but caught it in my pocket.

We talked about this guy we knew who wrote newspaper articles about richy people planning a brunch every Saturday. Bright young things, what my friend called the heroin-and-pasta set. I was wearing my long coat, it was cold out, so I couldn't decide to carry the guns in my outer pockets or my jacket ones. The best for carrying weapons I always thought was when I was in the Regs, the Reg Forces. Then you have a good holster, things have straps. It's not the same when you have your own weapons. They've got that right. Have to admit I kept my Belgian FN rifle cleaner than anything I've had since. Well, you had to.

A few years earlier I sat with the gun in my mouth, I was handcuffed. A porn movie was playing on the TV, I was 17 so I hadn't seen many. Lots of magazines, though. Before arriving at the junior common room we'd been told what elements of our uniform to wear. I had on my can, boots, and a toque. My hands were folded in my lap, natural-like, as if I wasn't cuffed. You switch the safety to "R" for rock & roll.

Earlier that day we'd been waiting to go for lunch outside the mess and a guy didn't make it to the can fast enough, his burst bladder darkened his pants as he marched.

I lay on my back, tense. It was how many sit-ups could I do in a minute. One guy'd told me not to do it, but it seemed like a good bet. They pulled the towel off my eyes and I leaned up, my mouth on his ass as the camera flashed.

Her friend wasn't dressed yet when we got there. Her brainy boyfriend, a guy I liked, passed me a beer. Oh so you've got a bit of a wound there he said, pointing at my stomach with the can.

I took it and opened it. Yeah, I hope this is dry. I poked at my stomach, it wasn't. It was hot in the apartment so I took off my coat, then my jacket, then my shirt and tie, pulling them over my head.

It was weird thinking that just being in this picture meant the Commanding Officer of the airborne regiment got canned. People were really pissed off at me after that, that's why I quit. I didn't have many friends, they started narking on me for stuff.

I shifted around on the couch. It was starting to get cool, it felt good. But my ass hurt from the cuffs on my back belt-loop. I get this little patch there from doing sit-ups & the cuffs were irritating it. I unlocked them and put them in the front. I didn't end up using them that night, though the next morning I whipped her as she swung around on my dick. She asked me, and I liked it a lot.

She was a witch, and she put a hex on me when we went out.

We ended up at some party, some guy's place with a brown corpse cake. The brainhead and I bet who'd puke on it first. He won. I smoked my filipino cigar I'd saved up and gave a light to anyone pretty who asked. Guy name of Dave asked me how I was feeling. We had this rhyme in the army: this is my rifle, this is my gun, this is for shooting, this is for fun. You never called your rifle a 'gun'. It was like calling a ship a boat. A gun was an artillery piece.

The guy in the car who laughed at me when we walked by was black, I think. I didn't take my guns out on the street though, this is the east side, you don't want to take any chances.

Later she sat around reading a book. I could just see the back of it, a guy looking at me, sitting on a pool table. He looked hungry and tired and cold. She'd carved a pumpkin and it was on the table, lopsided, furious holes with blood around them.

The thing about the pregnant teenie bopper though was her girlfriend wanted her to keep the baby. But she was a lot older. And when you're thirteen you've got your whole life ahead of you. She was going to put it up for adoption. Every once in a while I'd put a gun barrel into my mouth like it was a cigar. I'd wrap my lips around it 'cause I have bad enough teeth already and I don't want to chip them any more. »

«GET SMART»

I WAS WAITING at Cambie and Cordova for my connection when I saw Jimmy barrel across the street from the alley to behind The Churchill. He was running after someone with a stick. I mean, they both had sticks. And so, like, then he's just standing there by the car and this woman starts yelling at him. He says something and she says, well he pulled a knife on 'em. He whines a bit, then he goes to wave the stick at her, I mean he does, but you can tell he's more scared of her. He's got it like a baseball bat, whereas before he carried it in one hand over his head. I wonder how they didn't get hit by a car. After the excitement died down I stood around for awhile outside The Cambie

Hotel. It was sunny. I saw Pete and some guy across the street. He nodded at me, kept walking, I crossed the street, dodging traffic.

Hey.

Hey, how ya doin'?

Good.

You gonna come by the office. He wasn't asking, he was telling.

Yeah, maybe, I'm waiting for a friend. You gonna be there a while?

Yeah.

I didn't think I'd go there, I wanted to go see a movie. Okay, maybe I'll see ya.

Yeah.

Yeah.

He turned around.

Hey, good time last night.

Yeah.

Yeah, sorry I drank all your scotch.

The other guy laughed. Pete waved his hand at me. Don't worry about it. I crossed back over the street. Pete's good people. When I first got to town he set me up with a lot of people, getting work. That's all I wanted, just to get some steady work and some respect.

Before, where I was before down east, it'd been you had to have a straight job to survive.

Then I see Ken and head across the street to his car. A guy gets out of the seat next to him and gets in the back with another guy. Guy looks South American? Korean? Can't tell. Rough, shiny, seamed & ridged face. Ken's like sitting there eating an apple. He's got a bag there on the floor.

Hey how ya doin'? I climb in. Bob Marley's playing, Ken's wearing his tweed cap backwards, a few braids stick out, his Vuarnet silver plastic shades.

Good, good. He crunches the apple.

I pull two folded up twenties out of my pocket and put them on the dash.

There's some in there. He points at a cheque box on the floorboards.

I open the box and pull out a bag. Right, I've uh I've got one. I stick it in my pocket.

Hey what're you doin'?

Now, not much, goin' to a movie later.

Yeah? You wanna smoke a doobie?

Yeah, sure.

Okay. He pulls out, car behind us pulls into our spot. There's a park near here.

We drive around, he turns, we head down for the water. I guess we could start it up now. Can you get that pill box over there.

I look at the floor again, reach down, feel stuff and then an amber pill bottle. I dunno how I know this, but I'm thinking it'll be like what you get prescriptions in, right? So it'll be amber with the white top. I remember seeing them when I was a kid, my dad'd have one from the doctor & it'd have his name typed on it. I thought that was cool—personalized drugs. I pull it up, it has a Safeway logo on it.

Get out the big one, if there is one.

I open the child-proof bottle and look inside. There's a couple roaches and a joint. I pull it out and take the lighter. I pass it back to the other guy in the back. He's got a button on his jacket saying 'Bud or Bud', showing beers and a pot bud. Ken pulls the car into a parking lot, and we're facing the water. It'd be great just to go lie on the grass; I've got a headache from not having any coffee yet. There's that song, please rub my forehead, I feel like whining.

We talk about movies for a while. Ken likes cop movies though he was stoned when he saw *Reservoir Dogs* so he wants to see it again. The night before buddy went for Hallowe'en as a Dog. He never carried a gun, had a knife though. Talked about the cop shooting up, going really down.

They dropped me off and I wandered around, went to a bookstore and bought a couple Arab novels, then went to see the gangster movie. The guy kept complaining about lack of organization on the West Coast. Man I know how that feels. I thought about getting a track suit before heading home, but decided against it. My size, in one of those I'll either look like a mobster or a bloated hog. »

«DOPE MONEY»

HARRY AND ME and Jimmy went into the tourist money exchange. This girl behind the counter looked like a virgin Barbie and was singing some rap song. I thought maybe she recognized me, though I'd never been in there before. Maybe 80s Night at that club, The Twilight Zone.

Jimmy took the manila envelope out of his jacket pocket and put it on the counter. He started arguing with the girl about the exchange rate.

Harry growled at him, What's the problem?

Aw, I just know that if we go down the street we can get a better rate?

Who gives a fuck? So let's go down the street.

So we high-tailed it out of there to the Money Mart. This was convenient for me 'cause I could cash my cheque too. So I went up with Jimmy and I couldn't believe it when he told the girl behind the counter it was drug money. Yeah, he says, we're going to Thailand for a day, pretty cool eh?

I grabbed his butt hard and gave him a little cock and ball torture, pulling him back from the cashier's window.

What! *What?* He was squealing like a four-eyed computer geek.

What are you fucking—aw forget it. I went back up to the window and handed over my cheque. They asked me for my card but I didn't have it so they had to pull theirs from the file. I stuck my finger on the invisible ink pad on the plexiglass window and rolled it on the box that the girl stamped on the back of the cheque. She checked my thumbprint against my card and counted it out in hundreds for me.

You'll uh have to excuse my friend, he's just kind of excited about this trip we're taking. Good thing you're not the police.

Oh but I am. She smiled at me and my sweat dried.

On the way back to the car Jimmy asked me not to

tell Harry about his fuck-up but I had no choice. Harry gave him the back of his hand and kicked him out of the car.

Fucken narc, Jimmy yelled at me as I reached out to close the door. Harry, aren't you even gonna pay me? You fucking owe me man.

Harry looked at me. I didn't want to fork over some of my roll, I knew that was money down the drain, but I didn't have a choice.

Hey, thanks man. Jimmy was trying to suck up & get back onto the crew. No one on the street paid any attention to him sitting there by the parking meter, even the boosters steered clear. *Gung hai fat choy*, man. He was so pathetic.

Later we heard he was boozing it up at Graceland and saying he was going to take Harry out for kicking him out of the car and 'cause we weren't gonna take him to Thailand tomorrow. I tried to get a hold of him but there was no answer on the cell. Then Harry called me up, he'd heard of the dissing and he told me to get my gat and meet him at the Pink Pearl. I drove down to Kingsway and got the piece and five hollow-points from a safe in my grandmother's house. She was on her monthly trip to an Indian reserve in

Washington State to play the slots. They always give her a room by the elevator.

I'd just set my truck's car alarm when I saw Harry's creamy Jag pull in. He was all effusive, his overcoat on his shoulders like a regular politician. Sunny was driving and he brushed some coke off Harry's shoulder before getting out and locking the car.

So this dickless wonder thinks he can take me out hunh? The little fuck—blah, blah. Harry ranted on, sucking duck's feet and spitting the bones out onto the white plastic tablecloth. I drank my Coke and waited for him to get to the point.

He goes to Sunny, What's going on with your case?

Eh, not much. The guy did a statement thing where he said it didn't have anything to do with me being coloured.

Yeah like fuck. But Melissa's gonna be able to say she went there first and he was gonna give it to her, right?

Yeah but the problem is he'd already rented it anyway. So he was just leading her on.

Harry sucked back his scotch. Oh yeah? To get in her pants?

Yeah.

Yeah okay, don't worry about it. We'll teach that cunt to mess with your girl. But let me take care of this Jimmy fuck first, hunh?

Oh sure, Harry. I'm just—nice of you to take an interest.

Harry liked to let the law handle things and then step in with a pistol-whipping.

Ah, you're just lucky you got me in a good mood. Okay let's get Jimmy squared away. Where's he live?

When we got there Harry stalked the hallways.

Hey Jimmy you dumb *low-fun* where are you. Fuckin' *gwai-lo*, you think you can—you're a nobody, abso-fucking-lutely nobody, c'mon out and take it.

Jimmy came out of his apartment and started to say something and Harry shot him in the chest and throat and head. I threw up on Jimmy's Reeboks and then I went back downtown and threw the gun into False Creek. This nazi chick was sitting on one of those pebbled cement stumps, wearing sunglasses.

I'd driven over in my own truck. I hate that three people, two cars scenario, where you leave your car somewhere to go with someone else and then you're in Port-Fucking-Moody all the hell and gone and you've gotta take the bus or a taxi to get back and pick up your car. Once I had to shove my tin snips down this dog's throat to get my truck out of lock-up after we'd been overnight in Ladner working some deal. I was gonna have to testify against Harry on that one when it turned out they were mounties but the case didn't get to trial, lucky for me. Don't wanna die on the streets of Ladner, that's for sure. »

«WHITE YAKUZA»

I COULD HEAR Laurie squawking from the bedroom so I closed the door and finished making supper. We sat down and I drank a beer with the meal. I opened another and felt the food settle in my stomach as I made a joint from the roaches in the hotel. Maria tucked her legs under her ass and reached for the joint, pursing her lips.

I was going to go out with my man Colin to see some country and western. Maria stayed home, had to get up & go to work in the morning. It was raining like shit so I took an umbrella. When we got to the club the ditz at the door, doorman's girlfriend, let us in. Then we got the aggressive act from mister hamburger in a

T-shirt. After I got through I guess the bar manager said to Colin, He work for you? Halftime we went outside, I wasn't that enamoured of the idea, just to smoke a joint. Back inside, standing up front, the girls next to us half covered the stage with their orange drinks. One of them asked me if I was a bouncer and I wondered why I wasn't smiling. I thought of Maria stretching as she got into bed, Laurie falling asleep on her perch in the cage. »

«SKY TRAIN»

MY MAN MANDEEP GILL had pussy written all over his face in the Stüssy fake-graffiti script, right down to the dots over the u. He used to wear pussy on a T-shirt he got on Granville Street, but then he kept having to beat up guys at the club. Frat boy homies, Death Row or Raiders caps if they really did come from the ghetto. North Delta ghetto, of course, and these Sikhs got toughened dealing with the Surrey skins and the white-lace brigade behind 7-11s in Whalley Town. Now my man Munay has a tat and everyone but bikers stays away from a guy with pussy tattooed across his Punjabi nose.

Munay was trimming his goatee when I came by to

pick him up. I live just over the bridge, North Delta really. The real estate agent called it East Richmond to my mom seven years ago when she thought she could carry a mortgage on a disintegrating condo built over a PCB cesspool. Close to Ikea so there was always a steady supply of Jeeps and Land Rovers to steal when I was a kid. Not much opportunity for a thief these days there, only mini-vans with red mirror ornaments and who wants a minivan except the Angels?

It was Ian told me about bikers doin' drive-by's in a Dodge Ram Van. It's got a K-car chassis and handles worse than a Hyundai. But not even the pepsi's in Montreal're crazy enough to ride a hog over that Slurpee they call a winter road. Ian was out there last winter, visiting his kid brother who was doing computer science at McGill. Or at least that's what Sam & Mundeep's parents thought, anyway. I went to the party they had, it was a big family affair, and Mr. Gill rented a karaoke machine and cheered when Munay and I did some old school stuff. We even did a rap for his brother—"The first Gill at McGill!"

But Sam was really paying his way through drug dealer school by studying cop science at some motherfucking "CEGEP" in the burbs. Ian mostly sat around

Sam's big downtown apartment—guess they're cheaper'n fuck there 'cause of the separatist guys—

. . . yeah and he tells me guess the bikers are in some conflict over who got to provide drugs to the judges & cops, you know, I can't remember, and the pen, so they were blowing each other up. It's all cause crack's on its way out down east, they're getting some heroin good as Vancouver shit and everyone's got a woodie for it, so there's more demand for coke. I dunno, I can't remember. But anyway. My point is all the bike gangs tool around in mini-vans in the winter. And blow each other up.

That's pretty decent.

Yeah, not that they care, they're all stolen, right? Montreal's bad for that, fuck, my fucken brother had to get a club for his Audi because some fucking frog threw a brick through the window. After his stereo I guess. Ol' Jacques LaBloc was lucky, though, 'cause Sam's girlfriend's parents were over for tea so all he did was go outside & run the guy's hand along the window. Let him off with a warning.

No way, harsh dude.

Ah, fuck it, they're nothing there man, the other crew, not the Angels but the other ones, Rock something, the Rock Machine, they're just like fake.

What do you mean? Not a real . . .

No, it's weird, it's screwy, like they're just a bunch of guys who were doing this low level dealing, on the Plateau, to students and stuff, and the Mafia decided they wanted to use them. They're bikers, or they ride Harleys in the summertime, & they look like losers, but they're not really the Angels or Satan's Choice.

I looked over Mandeep's shoulder into the mirror. Pulled down the front of my Indian motorcycle jacket. I took off my Grizzlies cap, my hair was nice & kinky. Fuck I thought I'm starting to resemble my uncle but if I squinted in the mirror I looked like a Jew. I knew my Jewish gangsta history pretty good though, liked those guys back in the 30s in Montreal and New York, fuck everywhere, smuggling juice over the border. It was good to be wearing my Indian and a ball cap again. A big wedding on the weekend meant I had to dig out a suit and wear that for three days. Weddings are okay, at least the food is and if they get a decent bhangra MC. And they always have white guys as the waiters, and there's nothing like seeing your uncle beam as a gora fills his water glass. Payback for white trash or what, eh?

Uncle was giving me the lecture, same one he's used ever since I became the family juvie case. Mom freaked when I started making money off the local Chinese brats. Fucking rich shits thought a Mercedes was armoured. I like those trunk CD-players—nothing a crowbar can't take care of & less noisy than broken glass. But now everyone's got car alarms so you've gotta pack the earplugs. I have to admit I did like seeing my cousin. Her hair was so shiny it'd make me reach for my Oakleys & that was all brushing, motherfucker, not half a can a Turtle wax like uncle used.

Hey Guru wassup?

Cuz started calling me that after I accidently went to school when there was a test to do & scored a hundred on some IQ thing. This stumped the nice counsellor there to no fucken end 'cause he thought I should be in jail by now instead of getting into his sperm pool. The counsellor, Mr. Fung, called my mother in for an interview. At first she was ticked off 'cause she had to miss work. Then she got confused when he told her I really wasn't that smart after all. He called them multicultural variables. Guess he had to keep the windows of his Nissan open for the next week or two after someone pissed in the air freshner pyramid.

Eh, not much. I was scoping some blonde waitress and suddenly felt guilty.

She saw me though and laughed as she said, Hey, fuck that, wanna come over after the wedding & watch some video?

I was up for that. She was taking communications at Kwantlen. Had to watch videos for class. I thought that seemed as slack as reading a book for school but at least I got to watch some more interesting shit than *Die Hard* what fucking number ever.

The first video was about some kids dicking around in the snow. It looked really barren and cold where they were, kinda like Abbotsford. The other one was about this lady in India who kept getting fucked over till she capped everyone 'n did time like a real gangsta, all luxuries and newspaper headlines.

Once someone planted cuz's picture in the *Indo-Canadian News* for a beauty contest. At first I thought she'd win for sure but then when I saw how pissed she was I offered to go over & put her curling iron up the judge guy's nose.

Oh it's okay. You're sweet.

I kept the picture in my wallet for a while but it got lifted one night at a club. Mandeep and me were on a deal and I almost shit my socks until I remembered I had the stash in my car. The last time someone lost stuff for him he cut off their hands, and then 'cause the guy liked dipping his dick in the stuff—well, you can guess the rest.

No reason male circumcision should be any easier than what those rich fucks do to their daughters.

But Munay, you're not even Muslim man!

Don't matter. It's the principle of the thing bro, the motherfucken principle. »

«NIRVANA»

IN THE NEXT ROOM Danny's kids were watching a porn video. Guys with glistening chests and invisible body hair were pumping into each other. The soundtrack sounded pretty good for porn. I realized it was the stereo.

Hey, Reefer, I yelled at one of the kids, is that Tupac? He kept elbowing his sister. She pushed him back and kicked her leg with a lazy motion, the comic book fell to the floor. She jumped onto the shag and got back to colouring, doing the sky a wicked purple. Reefer got down with his sister and started in on a half-finished truck on the opposite page. It was the exact yellow of early '70s Tonka trucks that my brother had and I used to play with, when we were already too old.

Later I was on the bus with Steve going downtown. A Columbia Saturday night. Fight was on, Tyson was gonna kick ass once again. Like the T-shirt says, all who fear him. Or respect him, whatever. I'm kind of getting tired of the loser cruiser if you want my honest opinion. We went past this restaurant the bus always goes by, this black and yellow Nirvana sign, Nirvana Van as my buddy Steve always goes, singing it to the tune of "Hava Nagilla," *We're in Nirvana Van, man*! I told him I was gonna buy a car with my next paycheque. And I might. So we get down to the bar. It got crowded later with some punkers and shit, but we watched the fight. But I wasn't looking when I saw him get knocked down. I was looking at the chick over—and then I heard the guys yell and I looked back and I saw him fall again. I guess it was on the instant replay.

And did anyone really see him fall? 'Cause you know, it's just like, you know, Tupac not really getting shot and shit. »

«KOTEX OR TESTICLE TUCK»

DANIELLE LIFTED HER LEGS over her head, so her feet almost touched the bedspread. She slid a couple pillows under her butt, settling back down with a groan, her knees by her face.

I dunno, she said. I think I'm going to call in again tomorrow.

Well sure, may as well eh? Maria drank some wine. You gotta let it, you know, heal. She pronounced heal in two syllables, her voice bouncing Surrey-style up and down. I lay down on the couch next to Danielle's bed and put my head on Maria's lap. On the TV a guy with a hillbilly voice was talking about how Elvis wasn't ever the same after 1956. Or '57. I looked at the pictures of Elvis getting out of a limo, the guy talking about when Elvis's mom died. But my head was still in Maria's velvet lap and I couldn't tell from my sideways view if Elvis was dressed for a funeral or to go to a country club. His hair was a huge, Butch-Waxed pompadour bounced in the front like a truckdriver's, but really black. I blinked, my eyes felt like the rim of a Margarita glass. I listened for a bit to Danielle talk about her benefits, and then looked back at the show. Names, and words with big letters in the middle of them, were moving up the TV like the end of a movie. I pushed some of the bigger buttons on one of the remotes and the VCR came on and off and then the picture disappeared on the TV. Steve came in, stirring a stainless bowl full of little yellow apple slices.

He goes, Hey so d'you want to listen to some tunes?

Oh, right on. Whaddaya got?

He put the bowl on the floor and disconnected the grey cable that stuck out from the front of the low wall unit. He rolled up the cable and splitter and stuck it into a hole in the panelboard behind the couch. Down on his hands and knees in front of the heart monitor shape of Danielle's knees in the air, Steve pulled some green ammo boxes out from under the bed. They were fifty cal's, and the white stencils with symbols for ball and tracer made me nostalgic. Steve popped one open, uh let's see we got mostly classics in there right now but let's get, uh, here's some Miles and—he handed me a battered and cracked Metallica case, the plastic worn down by nights of work boots with exposed steel toes kicking CDs around the basement apartment before stumbling into bed, Danielle and her boyfriends and girlfriends partying on the bed in the middle of the room, watching the Power Hour on the late night rebroadcast before dropping a last butt into a full can of Kokanee and crashing. By the time Phantom Lord shuddered through the stadium-surround speakers we were all pretty baked, looping into conversational meanderings. I tried to get videos happening, but we couldn't think of a movie that had all the essentials, a car chase, torture, and the English countryside. Steve pulled out pictures from when he was in the Gulf, Arabs in flowing robes and a charred doll in the desert, gaunt and frantic strangers in a boat and the science fiction look of a city's midday freeways and office towers.

We ended up playing Scrabble and Maria won, not because she got 'ovary' or Danielle got 'coven' but just out of luck, the pale tiles turning over random letters that ended up as words, inching across the board and stopping at the edge. »

«EASTERNER»

BLONDIE CAME BY where I was sitting on the ground, cleaning my boots. I looked up at him in the harsh sun, a white-brilliant aura around his tall head.

Hey you want to get a coffee?

Yeah. I know someone who has some. Great idea. So how're you doing?

Oh you know. Campbell's great, the great benefactor.

Yeah he's like a factor. How's the place?

It isn't the ground. It's a funny part of town. Old. Older'n Ontario, eh, ain't that the fuck?

Yeah. So he gave you the lecture.

Yeah.

He grinned and almost tripped over a treestump in the middle of the road. We went into this place on the corner and I gave the order to the chinese lady in there. We stood around and I looked at some newspapers they had.

I drank some of the coffee right away when I got it. It was hot though. So what're you gonna do?

I dunno, mostly move stuff around.

Yeah? You're set up. The guy set you up?

Yeah. Cool, hunh?

Got any jobs?

What? He looked at me. You?

Yeah. What the fuck, I'm tireda being poor.

» » »

USUALLY I'D GET THERE in the morning & do the horse shit & then we'd ride somewhere & meet someone. Then we got a glass of beer. Then I'd go see my girl. There's guys in Toronto've painted her picture.

But when we met back there at an artistic party she'd been getting tired & wanted to come back here, settle down. So she's got this place & that's pretty well taken care of. And her son's here and that's proper.

When I got back she was sitting with a blanket on her. It was one her mother had made. We took our clothes off and got into bed. I scraped my knees on the floor licking her cunt and after she came she turned over and I fucked her. We lay together for awhile and then she got up. I got up too and threw some water on my face, rubbed her through her dress and started looking for something to eat. There wasn't much so I went to the Hudson's store for provisions. The next day I was shooting at tin cans when Gregory Campbell came by.

That mare looks like she was rode hard and put away wet.

Yeah, well, you know how it is Mr Campbell, gotta get inside. I couldn't stand the guy.

Listen you fuck, can you do me a favour?

Yeah sure what is it?

Oh it's just getting these guys in, over the border.

I coolied for a while doing that, then decided to cool it. »

«SLACKER»

I SPAZZED MY WAY OUT of anything at Basic Air Force training, going on forced marches in the truck, my "twisted" ankle wrapped in a gaudy grey stump. The flight sergeant was always bitching at me over my sideburns but me & Frenchie'd just pass a smoke back & forth, bouncing in the deuce-and-a-half truck drivin over the back forty in Moose-Fuckin'-Spit Manitoba. Back on base we'd spend the weekend jerking off, the springs a chorus of horny crickets. Dube got some reefer sometimes from his traitor gangster friends back in Montreal & we'd sit out back, talk about Sinatra, cruising the Don Valley back home, this great pair of bags he had.

Luckily the jew-hater bought the farm before the brass sussed it I was shooting so bad on purpose, and after demob I hit the rails for Van, figuring I'd get a nice safe job behind a counter 6,000 miles from Bomber Harris. It was a decent shop over on Boundary and I got a place and a girlfriend at Rupert & 25th 'cause Burnaby's too Limey for me and a '38 Buick I painted white 'cause with my complexion I look Mexican and I seen these hep cars the Cali zoot suiters drive in a Dorsey magazine.

Coming home from work in the summer of '55 I noticed a chicken in a Rambler next to me I seen buying a fan belt. Turned out she lived a block away and when she got home boyfriend, a sportswriter, was making supper, humming along to "Jeepers Creepers." I had a bottle of beer and looked at the Rat Pack and Burt Lancaster posters they got, we talked a bit about Joe Kapp and the Lions' chances this season. Then I walked home and saw my girlie strolling up the walk, this blue dress so her calves looked like fists ready to sock me one. My straw fedora she bought me at Spencers was damp around the rim, and I took it off and wiped my forehead with my arm. She stopped on the doorstep, took a pair of police handcuffs out of her little purse and said, "allons-y, allons-on." I bowed my head in pride and blushed in delicious submission. »

«DE LOSER»

GUY WEARING A brown suede carcoat pulls up to the curb in a Range Rover type Jeep—almost hit by this honking guy—he yells, walks over to the phone booth. Another guy crosses the street, also wearing a carcoat, walks past the booth into the Church's Chicken. Valentine's Day. His cell phone rings when he's in the line-up, he takes it out, walks out to the booth, shoots the guy, gets into the running Jeep, cranks the stereo, pulls out into the path of a gravel truck. »

«UNTITLED»

for Mark Laba

HYMIE WAS LYING ON his ex brother-in-law's daughter's bed, with the covers pulled up over him. Nek, Hymie's ex brother-in-law, stood above him rolling a joint. Nek was worried about Hymie because Hymie had sustained a really bad wound to his groin area, self-inflicted, and then passed out. Nek was also Hymie's lawyer and they were meeting at Nek's place to map out a strategy in an assault charge against Hymie.

Look man I told you.

I don't wanna fuckin' hear that man. Now look, what happened?

Look, it's like I told you.

What the fuck happened to me? Hymie was yelling now, his head leaning up a bit, stiffly, awkwardly. He pulled his arms out from under the covers. The counterpane was a nubby hot pink with fringes all over the place. Nek thought as he looked down at Hymie that it was ironic you couldn't see blood on a pink bedspread. The blood was just a dark glossy wetness where Hymie's legs met, the pink of a map of the British empire from back when Nek was in elementary school. He looked at his daughter's Virgin Mary nightlight next to the bed. She'd left it on all day. He'd have to talk to her about that.

It's like I told you, we were both really high from that weed.

That's the weed—

The weed my brother's friend's dad grows.

For his cancer.

For his cancer.

And so what, so I'm fucking high? So are you. You don't feel like you're getting a blowjob from a pitbull and you've got some bitch's tampon stuck between your teeth.

Which bitch is that? Nek was trying some humour here.

Which? Hey, there ain't no tampon man, it's a fucking figure of speech!

It's like I'm telling you, Hymie. Geez you don't listen too good anymore man. Think you've been smoking too much.

What? Yeah, yeah right. Like it affects your hearing. I need some, gimme some a that. Hymie gestured with a jerk.

Nek passed over the fattie he was in the process of lighting. Like I was sayin' Hymie, you better chill the fuck out. You smoke all that stuff, then you can't sleep, so you put in those earplugs you got and they push alla your earwax in then you can't hear and you turn up that walkman you got and then it's even worse.

Listen, fuck man! Nek tell me what the fuck happened here!? Hymie swept his hands around and down like a homeboy with wings. His eyes were watering from the smoke from the joint between his lips and his face was slick with sweat from the severe trauma he'd suffered half an hour ago before passing out.

Hymie, Hymie, Hymie, just cool it, okay. You fuckin'—Hymie, you fuckin' bit your own dick off!

What the? What what what what, what the fuh?

Yeah, yeah man, it's like I've been trying to tell you, we're like high right so we're miking the frozen veggie chili dogs Suzanne got and you start getting confused I guess, you went to the can like to take a whiz and I hear you scream, only it was a weird scream, like you were trying to talk with food in your mouth, sort of a low-pitched gargling noise, *urggharg h*, and I go in there and there you are, on the, with your hand, your head on the john and your fly is open and you've bit off your own dick.

Yeah those fuckin' chili veggie dogs. They're fuckin'—man I can't believe we were gonna eat those things?

Yeah well, but anyways, for your information it's veggie chili dogs.

What's the fuckin' difference?

Well 'cause like a veggie chili dog, that means it's a chili dog that they've made vegetarian by making it not out of meat. You know, whereas a chili veggie dog means it's a veggie dog they've added chili to.

Fuck, what the fuck? Fuck man you think too much. And I'm coming red here buddy!

Not as good as pissing white eh?

Fuck it's just, no, naw naw man. Hymie was trying to pull himself back together.

Fuck man, swear to fucking god. There was a horrible quality to Nek's memory, to seeing Hymie's smeared lips. He'd tried to clean them up with a facecloth.

How could I've? Fuck.

Fuck I don't know man, I don't know. You're—I don't know, you just ripped off your own dick man. And yeah you should just cool down man. If you don't mind me saying. 'Cause, like you know, you are the worst fucking recipient of bad news. If you don't mind me saying that, you know, no disrespect or nothing.

Fuck man! You are the—Hymie was closing his eyes a lot here, looking down. Look man I don't want to, I don't wanna. I can't look at it. Hymie still hadn't lifted up the covers. Fuck man it's caught in my throat.

What?

Fuck, it's caught in my throat! My own dick is caught in my fucking throat!

What? No, what? Nek leaned forward a bit, he didn't quite know the protocol here.

Fuck man I can't. Hymie jerked up from the bed. I can't. I can't breathe. He sounded like he was trying to take a shit or suck a popsicle.

Nek moved forward and put his hand on Hymie's forehead. It was kind of greasy but he remembered how effective the gesture was on *Trapper John, M.D.* Gonzo just waltzed in & did emergency surgery, had that wicked RV parked out in the lot, only time he ever saw an RV that looked cool. It was like the Vietnam vet of RVs, like a Hell's Angels RV. That guy Gonzo'd just sit back there on the roof, reading some french novel or some shit and drinking a fuckin' Singapore Sling in his Hawaiian shirt with some nurse babe over.

Hey man, Hymie man, you remember *Trapper John, M.D.*? You remember that show?

What? What?

You remember *Trapper John*, that show, where this doctor, Gonzo, he was this total slacker and he lived in this RV out on the parking lot?

No man I don't.

No, sure you do man. It was like—but he gave it up. What'd'you want? We got, I think I've got some coke. He wondered if coke was good for choking on your own dick. And bleeding.

Afterwards he felt even more useless. He opened the phone bill and wrote "don't go in there" on the envelope and taped it to his kid's bedroom door. He needed some fresh air. It wasn't 3:00 yet, and there were just a few pedestrians along the seawall in front of his condo. The sky was quite blue, with a milky edge and a smear of brown pollution. The tarp fluttering in the air made a nice steel-drum sound. But then something strange started happening. As Nek walked along, it became harder and harder to lift his feet up. Or rather, it seemed as if they were stuck to the sidewalk but also pulling it up. And the sidewalk actually was coming up with his feet, pulling up in a fabric or cartoon shape. The sidewalk around, and the grass even seemed to move toward the offending foot, as if the surface of the world was just one continuous layer detachable from what was below it. The leaves of the tilting trees rustled like it was really windy.

This made walking more difficult, and even as Nek developed a flicking gesture for each foot, which flicked off the sidewalk about a foot above where it originally was, the ground was still slipping around, and everyone around him looked like the extras in the *Godzilla* commercial, hands out to steady themselves, knees bent, faces thoughtful. As Nek walked along, the ground sucking to his feet, he came up to a guy working on a ladder. The guy was cleaning the second floor windows of the complex next to Nek's. His ladder started to teeter when Nek approached and Nek walked more carefully. The guy leaned his elbow on the window ledge and yelled out at him: Hey man, watch the fuck out eh?

Yeah sure, sorry, Nek said.

And stop dealing drugs in the neighbourhood, from an old woman who opened a window next to the ladder. Scum! She realized she was talking to a complete stranger and closed the window, jerking the sheer curtain shut.

Hey I don't—he tried sliding his feet, he could move that way. He slid over to a bench and collapsed onto it. The sailboats in front of him were pretty. They looked like a jigsaw puzzle if you took out the rollerbladers. A guy in a dinghy at a charter boat carefully lifted a portable TV set onto the larger boat. He was going to have to deal with the old lady later.

He thought about the coke comment he made to Hymie. He was glad he'd said that, it was a Christian gesture, he thought. 'Cause he really didn't even have any coke. They'd had the last of it on Sunday afternoon when they got back from having brunch with his grandmother out in the 'burbs. It was at a sit-down fast food restaurant, a regional chain that had upgraded a few years earlier, so instead of Model T's, the pictures on the walls were by some artist. He thought it was nice to give Hymie some hope about there being cocaine because maybe that made his passing into the other world a bit easier. Heaven was probably like cocaine. He thought about how he would phrase what happened to Hymie to his grandmother the next time they had brunch. He could probably tell her about a friend of his who passed away and then get back to the deal she got on her next trip to Reno. »

two

«ME & MOM»

DAD DIED WHEN I WAS 17. I was around the house all the time then, because I'd failed Practical Math for the third time lucky & just worked part-time at the old folks' home piling crappy food on the plastic trays for $5.75 an hour. Union. So when Mom asked me if I wanted to get married I said sure.

What we did was go to another part of town, down by the government buildings where the registrar was. And since Mom & Dad had never been officially married she had a different name than me & I was so wasted I looked 25 or so & Mom was pretty good looking for 39.

At least this way, I thought, she wouldn't be bugging me about cleaning my room any more since now she'd clean it anyway.

And this was true. Dad had been a real prick, or maybe that was just my impression of things ever since he asked me in front of my grandparents if I'd started masturbating yet. I was 14, so of course I had. Mom was quite the good one at keeping the house neat and tidy, and unlike when I was 'single', now that I was married I didn't have a room of my own. Not that I'm complaining. But before the wedding, my room had somehow become this real issue between us, kind of tacitly recognized as a semi-autonomous region like those parts of China where mongoloids come from.

So, first of all, it was pretty great. Mom seemed to mind less about making breakfast for me, it gave me a reason to get up in the morning & I stopped jerking off so much. I didn't really know anyone any more, all my friends stopped hanging out when I left Campbell Collegiate and the only one I knew at work was Frieda, the shop steward who used to be a nazi in Germany. She was really old, over 50.

I got into stuff like mowing the lawn on Saturday mornings, something my Dad never did before because he wanted to work on souping up his car. It's too bad he trashed the car so bad in the accident, but it was kind of neat sitting on the back seat of the bus with Mom, holding her hand like we were a couple of teenagers (well, one of us was, I guess), going downtown to buy some records, the Jam for me, Janis Joplin for her, & maybe see *Apocalypse Now*. This was dangerous, because lots of my ex-friends rode the buses too, but Mom'd started wearing cooler clothes, tight jeans & a light purple T-shirt with a scoop neck, so she wouldn't look anything like she used to when she was chained to the house.

But I needed a change & we both realized this. Talking it over one night watching *Carson*, we decided I should leave my job at the nursing home & look for work in a restaurant, where maybe I could start making fifty, a hundred bucks in tips. Mom told me I was good looking enough to get all the chicks & old ladies drooling over me. I don't know, it made me feel kind of weird for her to talk that way about it.

Later on, I got up to open the window because it was really stuffy and hot. I could hear the light hiss of traffic from a main street a block away, then the rumble of a streetcleaner brushing down the curb and pavement and sidewalk. I remembered then that the next day it was garbage day so I pulled on some pants and shoes and went outside to move the cans down the driveway. The 'driveway' was just two clay ruts in the grass, and up towards the house the oil from Dad's car had even killed the grass between the ruts. I came back inside the house, walking quiet so Mom wouldn't hear me, but she was standing in the doorway to our bedroom, one shoulder leaning against the doorframe, smiling as she told me she was proud of me for getting up & remembering the cans. I felt good inside from the praise, like the last time I'd brought home a decent report card. And that was a long time ago.

As it turned out, I didn't leave my job at the old folks' home. I liked it too much there, even if it was greasy and all that shit. I was only working part-time, on call. One day I came home from work, about 7:30, I'd been washing pots, which usually meant standing for eight hours in one spot, a Walkman on, and three layers of aprons. I kicked off my North Stars, orange and black suede ones, & they bounced against the hall closet. Mom was bringing a power tool out of the bathroom and she gave me a hard time about acting so sloppy. I yelled back at her & said I'd had a shitty day at work. She said that was no excuse & then her face all softened and she put her arms out wide and told me to come here.

» » »

The next day, I got up about noon and the curtains are still drawn across the window but Mom wasn't in bed. I heard the house groaning and sure enough she's out back with the heavy black garden hose, hooking it up to the water sprinkler, or trying to. I just had my little adidas shorts on, the red ones for gym, but I came out, it's already pretty warm. I grabbed the sprinkler and made the final connection and the water stopped frizzing out all over the place.

Mom looks really hot even when I just see her there bending over the hose end and the sprinkler. It feels kind of weird to say that your Mom looks 'hot'. Like, 'hot' is something you say about a girl at school whose jeans are really tight and you can see her snatch or when you're standing on the bus and this punk chick puts her arm up to hold onto the railing and you can see the hair in her pit. You know, Visible Panty Line, stuff like that. But my Mom, that's a different story. I have to realize, I think to myself, that maybe it's always been that way.

When I was seven was the only time we ever went on a vacation. My Dad decided he was going to drive all over Western Canada, all the way to Winnipeg via Saskatoon & then back to Regina & Calgary and the Rockies and then across B.C. to Vancouver and then back the Yellowhead route to Edmonton and then home. So we boot it all over the place, me playing chicken running through the woods in whatever fucking National or Provincial park we're at, tripping over roots & running into big trees that cut my forehead fearsome. Meanwhile, Mom & Dad are at the tent-trailer, Dad trying to tune in some baseball game and Mom cooking weiners on the Coleman stove. I come back all throbbing with pain, my face scraped white, my ankle twisted, whatever. At one of these places they had a lake, well, probably at most of them they did. At some particular one, since I can only remember this happening once, we were down at the lake. Probably a five-minute walk through the community of like-minded campers.

Mom and I were at the lake and Dad was back at the tent-trailer, listening to the Cubs get scalped by the Tribe. Mom had one of those floral swimsuits, with a panel across the front and thin straps like twine that got caught on her knobby shoulders. So Mom was picking me up and 'dropping' me in the water, I say dropping in quotation marks because she never lets go of me, and as she puts me down my hand pulled at the panel between her breasts, the spaghetti straps tighter than ever on her shoulders, this particular look on her face, baseball widow and a tight, tight grin. »

«HAMLET»

I DECIDED: I want to get back into my mother's womb. I phoned her up to communicate something to that effect. I called after 11, so it'd be cheaper.

She was doing the dishes my Dad said, they're like that, you understand. Dad & I chatted for awhile about nothing in particular. I've never been able to talk to him about much, not about politics certainly, since he's voted Liberal since the days of Diefenbaker. It was now about ten after 11, & I had the TV on with the sound off, Arsenio Hall was wrapping his legs around each other and making his thumb fit behind his first knuckle. Then my Dad said here she is & he put my mom on the line.

I asked Mom how she was. Fine & her voice sounded puzzled because I usually only call on her birthday or Mother's Day. Special occasions. So I gave her the scoop. Told her I wanted to get back in her womb. The whole story was I was being evicted from my apartment as of the end of the month, the landlady's cousin was moving in and I didn't have anywhere to go, anywhere appropriate. Mom was a bit nonplussed. This was coming at a bad time. She was going on two days computer training next month, Lotus 1-2-3 & she didn't see how she could fit me in.

This was not going the way I intended it, right? It's not like I want to move back in with my folks, I want to move into Mom. She says let's be practical. My Dad pipes up on the phone, saying now let's look at this from your mother's perspective. Think of what she'd be going through. I don't see how it's such a big deal. I can't afford to live on my own, not in this city, so why not? I've had some set-backs. Between opportunities. These, these recessionary times.

Mom relents like I always knew she would. I say great. We made our plans. I was to get a hold of her in a day or two. I gave her to understand that this was just a temporary hold-over, till I got back on my feet again.

Next day, I made some calls and tracked down a friend who had some space in his basement where I could store half my stuff. I took it over in two taxi rides, no real furniture, a dinette chair and a mattress that flopped out the back of the cab's trunk. I decided to keep my little portable TV I got for $90 at the Safeway years ago. Mom's probably cable-ready.

I showed up on her doorstep with my Adidas bag in hand & my TV under my arm. Dad opened the door, I gave him the brush-off. Mom was upstairs in the bedroom, ready to recieve me. I came in & she opened her legs. Right away she nixed the TV. I figured I could live without it, do finger puppets or something. Inside, it was darker than I expected. I pushed my bag ahead of me, & left my runners outside after I got my feet in. It was real comfortable. There was a soft glow, pinkish, coming in through her stomach. Or I guess it's her abdominal wall, Grade Nine Health class came flashing back. Then I was startled by a booming-soft noise, it was Mom talking. She was talking to me, asking how I was getting along. I told her I was just fine. I pressed my mouth up against the wall and made that blubbering sound parents do on their baby's stomach. Mom giggled, a medium-pitched rumble, and sighed and patted on the other side of where my lips and nose were.

I curled up to get in a comfy position, like I was on my couch watching TV. Then I had this sickening thought—had I dragged that old couch out of the apartment building & down to the curb? I fell asleep in the cabride over to Mom's place, and maybe I dreamt it. I'd tried to clean up the apartment as best I could, because I wanted to get back as much of my deposit as I could. There was a minute or two of tension, then I relaxed. When you're back in the womb it's hard to really get uptight about anything.

I feel so good in here! You know? There's really nothing like being home at last. It's been three, four weeks now, I'm losing track of time, like some guy in a Solzhenitsyn novel, only this is a prison I like.

Back to my first day.

Mom was really considerate too—as Moms always are. She went downstairs to get a snack. Probably knew I hadn't eaten for days. I heard a door open and close softly, and the crisp rattle of a stiff plastic bag. She was taking some slices of whole-wheat bread out of the freezer. She keeps it there because she doesn't eat it fast enough. In a few minutes Mom was eating tea and toast. I felt my strength come back almost right away. I was grateful.

Now was sack time. Mom was back upstairs on her bed, watching TV. She had her hands crossed on her belly so the light was very dim. In a few minutes, the beat of her heart lulled me to sleep, like a cheap clock will a new puppy. I had pleasant dreams, imagining I could hear the blood around me in her abdomen, being gently rocked when she stood up to get something. Getting little hard-ons, but no wet dreams.

After that soothing start, the next day was a bit harsh. It was a Sunday, so in the afternoon Mom sat around out back on a reclining lawn chair while Dad fired up the barbecue and made some steaks. His famous twenty-minutes-a-side well-done specials. But it was really sunny out, so really bright and hot inside where I was. After awhile, I don't know how long, I must have started to get sunstroke, because I got real paranoid. First thing, I thought I could hear Mom's skin frying from the sun. It's crazy of course, but you're a bit cut off from the world when you're in the womb, to say the least. I felt like a piece of meat left in a bag of groceries in a hot car. Then, whenever Mom turned over on the lawnchair to lie on her side or front, I could swear I could feel the criss-cross of the straps pressing into me through her stomach. More than once I took a damp face cloth out of my gym bag and wiped my face.

Later that night was a bit better. After the meal, which I didn't really appreciate, being so hot and sticky, the night cooled down, and Mom just sat there drinking Long Island Iced Tea. I felt nice, cool and cheap. Then she got up and said she was going in to get a sweater. When we got inside she went up to the bedroom, closed the door, and took out a book to read. After maybe ten minutes, she fell asleep.

I was beginning to wonder if I was coming between my parents, which was not my intention at all, really. I lay in there for awhile, thinking of this, but fell asleep before I could see if Dad would come upstairs.

When I was in high school there was this drama teacher, Mr. Fortescue, and he said that one of the purposes of drama was to work out problems in society, and he said that even doing a puppet play about something that's bothering you could help. This, after awhile, I thought would help me here. I thought I couldn't have been the real cause of my parents drifting apart. The next day, Mom's at work and I tried to suss it out, couldn't. So what I did was do a little puppet play, only I didn't have any socks, since I was naked in my mom's womb. So I took out a pen from my gym bag and marked little faces on my fingers, one for Mom, one for me, one for Dad.

Dad is the thumb & he's pissed off. Mom, the index finger, is treating him carefully. I'm at the end of the hand, the pinkie. The idea is I try to stop Mom and Dad from fighting, but I get hopelessly entangled. Meanwhile, this is all to no avail, at least not what I intended. My finger puppet play's tickling my Mom from inside. She's at work and laughing like crazy, her prosthetic son inside, making her laugh and rubbing her tummy like she took care of him when he was a baby. »

«MY DAD'S WOMB»

I SAID TO HIM, Dad you're a fucking whore. And he said, What do you mean son? He's sitting there on the patio out back, triangular piece of cement laid in at the corner of the sidewalk to save the grass. Now there's just dead topsoil under the cement. In the driveway there's my dad's womb and some guy dad knew from work was getting out of it.

Dad goes to me, you know, that man once told me he thought you did a really good job shovelling snow from the driveway. Dad knows him from work. He comes up to us, pulls a balled-up Laurier bill out of his pocket and throws it on the picnic table. Dad made the picnic table with the instructions you get from the

Canadian Tire. I held the circular saw and thought about some guy who called me out at school and in a couple of weeks we had a great table for anything but eating on since the forks always fell through the slots and no more than one person could sit on either side or the whole fucker'd tip over. But that's alright, really, since it's just me and dad anyways. Hasn't always been this way, but it always might be, you never know.

There was a beer strike on so we were drinking Olympia from the States and the guy, his name was Les, stayed and had some with us. I got up in a minute and went inside to change the record on the stereo. I was buzzed so I didn't give a fuck and I put on "Rock Lobster" and dad throws a hairy fit as soon as I get out the door—*turn that garbage off*! He made these speakers for the stereo, ran cable outside & they look like the PA's in school only no knob underneath and spraypainted a glittery green-gold so I went inside, turned it off, and went down to my room to continue my porno novel about my english teacher with the stumpy fingers.

My dad's the real documentation one and he wants to actually sell the idea for his womb to Detroit and he made up the literature for it and everything. The specs are it has 88 hp, strut suspension, 148 lb curb weight,

2 valves a cylinder, adjustable steering column, all the head/legroom you could want. A little later I turned off the Flying Lizards from my Sears special am/fm stereo turntable 8-track system and went back upstairs. Les was gone and dad was snoring so I went out into his womb. It's all steel and shiny on the outside but lined with good quality dupont acrylic fur on the inside. I lay down and pictured what my wife'd look like one day when I got one and wondered if she'd smoke. I'd had this crush one time on a girl in grade ten, and at Valentines Day when everyone could send each other a carnation for a buck, I got a pink one from her. I took her downtown the next week when we had to go see a play at the university that had guys with huge hoses coming out of their pants and the women were on a sex strike to stop a war, or start one, or something. I was pulling into some fucking parking garage and I'd just got my license and I was driving my mom's Chevette and I told this chick *I didn't know you liked me that way* and she called me by my name and said that someone was playing a joke on both of us. *I never sent you the flower*. It seemed more like a joke on me and I smucked the car door into a pillar and when I got home that afternoon I went to the convenience

store my mom worked at and wore a Nixon mask and had dad's SMG and blew everyone away including my mom, but I was never caught for some reason.

In my dad's womb I was thinking about this but it was very relaxing. The bass throbbed a bit too annoying, but they always do with anything that isn't factory, you noticed that and the revery completed my ecstasy. I could just hear from outside, planes making the big turn for the descent into the airport, planes from far away places like Saskatoon or Kelowna. Then there was this rocking and ruckus and the door went open and dad was standing there about to give me shit for smoking up in his cunt. He throws a fist at me, what the fuck you doing here, he says. I could have someone coming by any second and you're the fucking hippy. I said to relax and take a pill. He wasn't really a redneck. Once when I'd been on my own for a couple of months and decided to come back home, this was when I was twelve, I guess, I had a couple of ounces and he helped me divvy it up and sell it to some of the guys in maintenance.

But I had to vamoose anyway. The site priority was to paying customers. Like I said at the outset, dad's a pro. »

«CROTCH SHOT»

COUPLE OF WEEKS AGO my sister called me up to see if I wanted a photograph of my mom. It was taken when I was sixteen, I mean when my mom was sixteen, she was ready to go to a dance at high school. We don't have any other pictures around. Our dad is blind, so he was never one to take pictures. I mean our dad literally here, he's my dad and my mom's dad. But not my sister's dad, some guy who stuck around for about five minutes by all accounts.

Maybe I should backtrack. But it's pretty difficult, you know. How can you ever figure out what happened in your family? Especially when you haven't met half of them. My mom was born out east and she moved around a lot with her mom. Her dad left them right after, and my grandma moved to wherever she could get work, mostly doing laundry. After about ten years she saved enough money to buy a rooming house here, down where they have the big houses near the old bridge. They were all run down, but she got these guys to fix up the place a bit, nail down some boards, and she bought half-a-dozen iron beds the army base was getting rid of. One of these guys hung around a lot and he and my grandma got married. There was lots of danger for women on their own so he protected her I guess, even though he couldn't see or nothing. But not my mom, because they got it on as well, quite soon after this guy and my grandma got married. That led to me, and when my real dad/granddad found out my mom was preggers he put his toe through a 30-30, resting his chin on the little blade at the top of the barrel. It's hard to shoot yourself when you're blind, kind of a handicap. I hear that they have lawn bowling for blind people, but they probably haven't gotten around to skeet shooting or target practice for them. My grandma never found out her dear departed husband of six months had made her daughter pregnant, so I guess dad wasn't blind to everything.

I'm in this picture too, although you can't see me because I'm about a month old in my mom's stomach. But I don't know, was it me? You know, all that biology stuff, how do people get made? My dad killed himself a month after the picture was taken. What did the shock do to my mom? How did it effect her? She started drinking lots, I know that, and a doctor told me that's why I don't have a groove in my upper lip. And whenever that cunt Cunningham picks me up for dealing I say that to her too: hey c'mon honey, I'm a 'fatal' alcoholic syndrome, see, I got no groove, can I see yours? Women cops are the worst, well, not back at the station, just when they pick you up. It's like they've got something to prove, right?

So my dad fucked up me and my mom. Big news, if he'd stayed around he probably would've beat her up so she'd lose me. It's better this way anyway. But my point is, in that picture my mom's quite a babe, in a jail-bait kind of way. I could really go for her. That's what I told myself yesterday when I picked up some little Indian chick at the bar, that it's my mother. Like I've never done it before, although now I know. I was having a beer at the counter, watching some trucks go through the mud on the TV. Sally, who was wearing nice tights and black runners, sat next to me and asked me slowly for a drink. She was talking so slow 'cause she'd been on crack, coming down from it. She wasn't going through the treads on her sneakers or anything to see if some fell in there, but she was stoked. So I got her a beer and Jim came in, the asshole. I owe him too much money, but I told him, if I can't sell some, how can I pay you?

Now the trick here is to know that he hadn't passed me the dope to sell yet, right? No, let me get this straight. I wasn't going to sell for Jim, we were just talking about stuff. This movie he saw where these guys had these guns to sell, something like that. Sounds like my life story. Get shot for something you wanted to do but never got around to. Except I've only been shot at. There's a difference, it's called feeling good when you cough up a lung in the morning. I need this haircut because I have to go to court tomorrow, which is the real drag. That's why I'm telling you all this.

They don't like you in court with long hair, and if you have it, you got to neat it up like the lawyers, except the lady lawyers, or the judges, only mine ain't white. But I'm talking to Jim on one side of me and

Sally on the other. She's not wearing a bra. Needs to, isn't though. And Jim passes this bag of dope over to Sally, why I don't know, but right then she has to go to the little girls' room. And then I feel Cunningham's fat hand on my shoulder.

Lady cops're all dykes, right? Just like in the army, everyone knows that. I was in the army for a week, went to Camp Corn-hole, that's what we called Cornwallis. It's down east, guess that's why it's full of fucking east coasters and frenchies. Threw myself down the stairs to get out. It was a good week, I had booze and weed every night because everyone wanted a tattoo and I could do them pretty good then, and I was twenty, so I was older than most of the guys. But all the chicks there were already tough, tougher than the guys, and you could tell they were lesbos. That's why I limp like this, because my ankle got chipped. But I got out.

She asked me what I was doing, and I said just sitting here constable, enjoying an alcoholic beverage. I offered to buy her one. And she asked me soft, what's in the bag. I'd stuck it in my shirt pocket when I smelled her, or maybe in my jeans, I can't remember, but she must've seen me. Down at 42 Division of the

Metro P.D. I tried to explain it to the detectives. They didn't bother acting like they cared about me, which I appreciated, but I didn't know them too well and I could've appreciated some bullshitting along that line after they were finished hanging me out the window. They thought I knew something about some killing, usual bullshit they pull on you when really they just want to jerk off in your face for awhile. 130 grams of dope. Fuck.

When I was sixteen I quit school and got a job stripping the wax off Chrysler showroom floors. A friend of mine asked if I wanted to sell some acid for him, and I said sure. He gave me 25 hits, blotters, and said to pay him 25 bucks in three days. I could charge what I wanted, probably two or three a hit. I wanted to try it, so I took four when I went to work, figuring I'd sell the rest after work when I was partying with some guys. I started flying and took four more in a couple of hours. That week I maybe slept three hours, but I kept working so I could pay him off. Didn't need a Walkman, fuck, didn't even have them back then.

I came home on Friday night, to go out again, and my mother was crying, drinking gin out of a bottle, watching cartoons. That was when she told me about my dad. Here's his address she said, giving me a piece of paper from a cemetery about five miles out of town. But I left the paper in my jeans and I guess she washed them. »

«CHALK CIRCLE»

YOU COULD GO TO Canadian Tire. Did you think of that?

Yeah. He put the food on the table. A woman outside the window asked Roberto, her youngest son, to give her the towels. A woman wailed. The walls in their kitchen were covered in images, ugly, torn from magazines or found on the street. A beetle which had eaten the cockroach chalk around the fridge was dead, its legs visible in the tile.

They drank wine out of coloured glasses with long stems: they were like girls in their mother's high-heels, salt-shaker stars in their hair. The glasses wobbled on the table's surface. She sucked at something in her teeth. He felt sluggish as they walked to the front of the apartment. A smacking sound came in the window, the greasy smell of meat.

She lit a stick of incense in the hallway.

I think I'm just going to roll one. Hunh, well. She opened a curved box on the footlocker.

You want some money for buying it? He took out his wallet, and looked at the bills in it.

Yeah, and for the emotional damage too. He gave her twenty-five dollars. Okay, 'cause you know—

Listen babe, you said we were smoking too much, and you didn't want to be doing it three times a day you know, what with going to school, and all weekend. And so we cut back.

Yeah, well, you know, because I was just getting into the party atmosphere at school today. Mr. Toth had a rum and coke.

Yeah?

Yeah and Andrea bought him another one but he left it. And Andrea said it was 'cause he knew if he finished it, that'd be it. Two drinks does it to anyone, she said. Oh just a sec, I'll get the picture from the party. She put down the wooden circle with indian designs on it and a sprinkling of dope.

Here it is. She came out of the bedroom with a wilted picture in her hand. He looked at it. It was from a party a couple of weeks before at these two lesbians' apartment in Scarborough.

Yeah, those boys sure were excited.

What do you mean by that?

Oh, whatever. He scraped the dope onto a rolling paper with a matchbook. He licked it and lit up. Umm, thanks for getting this. What'd you do, go home? He took another puff and passed it to her.

No, yeah. I went to, I came home. I was home till 5, when I got your message.

Yeah, then you went out?

No, I was out when you phoned I guess, and then I came back. I'm so glad you were still there when I came over. That's when I thought of Crappy Tire.

We could go there. I mean, I could go there to get an adapter for that pump?

Yeah.

He got up and put a tape in the ghetto blaster. The Beasties came on, mid-song, loud. He turned it up.

Yeah that was great seeing you. You just looked so happy there. He thought of seeing her on her bike, coming up the street to where he was drinking with

Jen and Pete. So how was Gary?

Okay if he'd just stop asking me to sleep with him.

Oh he did that? He picked up the roach clip and fastened it to the joint. He drew deeply on it. The music said, she's crafty.

He was sitting on a sagging green armchair, made of nylon fabric. Its feet had disappeared years ago. She sat with her legs crossed, pink cutoffs pushed up her white thighs, on the futon couch. She sat on a red blanket. Yeah. So it was nice seeing Pete and Jen.

Yeah, nice seeing them out of their house. Yeah, too bad he didn't come to the movie.

Yeah well, you know. Isn't the picture hilarious?

Look at Harvey's grin. He looks just fucking crazy.

Yeah wasn't he hilarious?

He stood up and walked out of the room. He took a piss, and splashed water on his face. The song went on about girls to do the dishes. He thought he could hear AC/DC from out the window. In the kitchen, he took a beer out of the fridge. You want a beer? he yelled down the hall.

No.

He went into the bedroom and opened a drawer in the cardboard nightable. He closed the drawer and slid a pair of handcuffs into his back pocket. She was spraying plants when he walked back into the living room. She turned around and slid her free arm around his waist. Hey there stranger. Nice package. Her hand slid down onto the bulge formed by the cuffs and her eyes widened. Maybe later.

He lay the cuffs on the footlocker and straightened up, kissing her on the mouth for seven seconds.

Mmm she said as he pulled away, showoff. He walked into the kitchen. She followed, and moved in front of him to use the sink. »

«RECREATIONAL»

ONCE I THOUGHT of playing hockey, chasing cocaine and pucks like ghosts in a Parkdale television set. I played for a couple of years, but I wasn't any good and not really into it. For awhile, I played baseball: same thing.

When I was twelve or thirteen my Dad bought a tent trailer. I think after I left home he got a hardtop, then later a trailer. He got an R.V. last year.

At Christmas, when my little sister went to a food-bank to get a toy for her kid, they gave her a turkey and vegetables and stuff. So she invited a lot of people over for dinner. Most of them were in construction, or casual, day labourers who get jobs through temporary manpower. They had some good dope and we sat around till late in the night smoking and listening to loud tunes. Her roommate Dan was in Hawaii with his parents so I got his room. He had a sagging waterbed. I got up a couple of times and went to the bathroom.

In the morning my sister's boyfriend Terry was already up and feeding the baby. Yeah he's a pretty good kid, eh? The night before he'd been feeding Jesse, the baby, in the kitchen, three or four guys circling around the kid and his mother's boyfriend, like emaciated pit bulls around a beautiful flower. Terry was boasting about how once they took Jesse into the emergency when he fell and hit his head.

Yeah and so he's a regular little trooper, weren't you? Last night, he wiped some orange baby food off the baby's chin as he said that. Talked about how he didn't cry. Now he smiled as he put out a cigarette in the clean ashtray.

I needed caffeine. It was my sister's place so I acted like I lived there. I made some coffee and poured a cup and took it into the living room. The centrepiece was a large glass coffee table, trimmed in brass, in three stacking circles that swung out. I put my cup on the smudged dark glass and sat back in the corduroy couch.

Jane, my sister, came tumbling down the stairs. Hey, I didn't get a chance last night to say it, good to see you.

Hey, of course I'm gonna want to see my sister at Christmas. It was nice to see her. I hadn't for awhile.

So what do you guys want to do? Terry came out of the kitchen, digging a pack of smokes out of his jacket pocket. He opened the pack and it was empty.

I don't know, maybe hang out for awhile? Terry looked at Jane.

Sounds good. You want some breakfast?

Naw, I'm okay.

Oh okay. Hey, did you see the art that Yvonne's done? She's really talented. Jane picked up a heavy carving that lay on the clutter of CDs and tapes next to the stereo. She passed it to me. It was shaped like a double-ended dildo, and had thousands of fine inscriptions, as if insects had worn highways and cloverleafs in the dark wood.

Pretty good.

Terry asked Jane for some smokes and she passed a deck over to him.

So did everyone get out of here last night?

Hunh? Jane looked at me, amused. Yeah you were

pretty wasted, eh? Bet you don't even remember. You were giving everyone a hard time about being my harem or something.

I drank some of my coffee. Hunh, d'you think they were pissed off?

No, of course not. Yeah, pretty much everyone was out of here by five.

I looked at my watch. It was ten-thirty.

So it's looking less and less like I'm going to work today, Terry said. Gettin' less and less likely, anyway.

Aw you should take the day off, Jane said, perching on his knee. Terry's face was wide and open, and on his right hand, which held Jane at the hip as he held a cigarette in the other hand, there was a tight white web of scar tissue, across half the back. Later, he told me about learning a lesson about not working stoned. Not using power tools.

» » »

AFTER WE GOT BACK from downtown Jane took me around to look for some mushrooms. We drove around in Dan's beater, a fifteen-year-old Toyota with a layer of coffee cups and cigarette packages covering the floorboards. Jesse sat in the back, gurgling and drooling some white paste and shit in his hand as he smeared it over his chin and the padded purple carseat.

So guys, I could hear her say from across the street, you guys got any 'shrooms? Yeah my bro's here for Christmas eh? I stretched out across the front seats, my dirty air Jordans out the driver's window, the back of my neck leaning against the cracked rubber on the passenger's door. My eyelids felt heavy, and I looked at the guys around the pick-up across the street. Jane was standing close to a tall guy in a sheepskin-lined jean jacket, pushed open by his gut, which rested on a silver belt buckle. Another guy was lying under the front end of the truck on a piece of cardboard. The front yard of the house had trees of all kinds, different sizes and colours, some with needles and some bare. I felt the cool West Coast air on my greasy forehead.

Hey guy, I turned to the back, how ya doin'? Jesse was playing with a bright red and yellow rattle thing, the mould flashing still present on the edges. He banged it against anything he could reach. You want some money? The glove compartment door had disappeared years ago, I guess when Dan had his stereo ripped off: comes from having a Kenwood decal on a piece of shit like this. I pulled a wad of Canadian Tire money out of the box. I hate the way when you see it on the floor at the mall or in the can at a donut shop, it looks like real money, like an old one-dollar bill maybe, and then you bend down & it's that Scottish shit. »

«FREE COUNTRY»

SIMON PASSED THE JOINT over to Maria. Mmm, no thanks. That's enough for me. I hate it when the filter, when the cardboard gets all . . .

What you mean you don't like the grey rotting soggy cardboard? How could you?

Yeah, well, anyway. Indian music played.

There was this guy, Simon goes. There was this guy at work today, name of Hal, and he goes—we were talking about free trade or whatever—and he goes, he's a real asshole, going on and on about something and I just felt like saying fuck you, you know what I mean?

Hmm. You wanna go into the bedroom? She rubbed her fingers on the palm of his hand.

Uh, yeah, unh-hunh.

She pushed up her top and reached a hand inside.

Whatcha doing? Showing off your bellybutton.

No, just—and she pulled a bra-strap over one arm, then the other. She moved over quickly and sat on his lap. Mmm, this is nice. They necked for a couple of minutes, then he stood up. She squealed delightfully as he twirled her around. He had a bit of a head-rush from standing up quickly and from the dope and from the Indian music. He squinted a couple of times, wetting the rims of his eyes, and let her down. She bent over the table and blew out the candles.

He stretched out between her legs and pulled down her jeans. She still had her tank top on and she leaned back on her elbows, watching him. He drooled onto her lips and began licking them slowly. His mouth was very wet and soon so was she. He kept licking her, trying different tongue and teeth techniques, biting, penetrating, stopping something when she flinched and pushing his face hard into her cunt when she moaned. He rubbed his face from her asshole to her clit, licking everywhere. She pushed his head away and he moved up next to her, kissing her with his face still wet. She wrapped her legs around him and pulled his body against hers. He put two fingers into his mouth and put them between her legs, sliding them down her clit and lips and into her. He moved back down to bite her hair, and slid two more fingers into her. He curled them inside her.

He rolled over and she sat on him, grinding her hips against him. She bent her head over his cock, drooling onto it and then moving her hand up and down it. She took some lubrication and wiped it on his ass, sliding two fingers into him. Then she flipped him over and sat on his ass, rubbing herself against him. She picked up the whip and flicked it gently on his back, then harder, raising red welts and he bucked under her.

Then she turned him over and grabbed his cock, sliding it into her cunt. He kept still, his hands folded behind his head, as she fucked him until she came. Then he pushed up into her, as she kept coming. She lay on him, shivering in small spasms. He rolled out from under her and lay on her ass, penetrating her and fucking. He panted after as he lay on her, their sweat cooling in the breeze. He rolled off her.

Pass me some Kleenex? They lay together for awhile, then she stood up and moved to the window, looking at the traffic. A tall guy across the street approached the corner, he wore an orange safety vest and a turban, his grey moustache flat against his cheeks from the strap.

She turned around and looked at the empty bed. She bent over and grabbed a sheet and tossed it onto the bed. He walked in, and stopped to pull on his shorts. Well, if that was breakfast that's it.

Hey, did you want something to eat?

Yeah, that'd be great.

Ok. He turned around and walked to the kitchen.

So you wanna get some tunes going here?

Yeah. She pulled a blue plastic milk cart out from under the table, and looked at the cassettes. She took one out and got it into the ghetto blaster. Aretha Franklin filled the small kitchen, and the phone rang. Up, oh, all get it.

He put two slices of bread into the toaster oven, and sliced some cheese.

She picked up the phone in the hallway. Yeah, Candace? . . . Oh not bad. So what are you up to? . . . Yeah sure. Okay, yeah, sure, come on over . . . Yeah okay, see ya. She hung up the phone.

So's she coming over?

Yeah, you want some juice? Yeah she thought she had to work today, but it turns out she didn't.

Oh yeah, so what's she up to?

Well anyway, yeah she wants to come over. We were thinking of going out, look at some fabric stores. Or she wants to, anyway.

Fifteen minutes later when they heard the knock she said, Coming. She hurried down the hall and opened the door. The hall was narrow and she knocked a Kewpie doll off a nail on the wall. Oh, just a sec. She picked up the doll and put it on the bookcase.

Candace came in and they hugged. So how's you guys doing?

Oh pretty good, we were just having some lunch. You want something?

Yeah, you want a beer or something?

Oh yeah, I guess so.

He opened the fridge and pulled three beers out. He twisted the tops off and passed two to the women.

Oh, so's you don't got any cinq-oh, eh? Candace laughed.

They walked into the front room. No, what is that, oh, you mean 50? He wondered if his face still smelled like pussy juice.

Yeah, that's what we used to call it, cinq-oh. Or

cinq-oh cinq-oh, you know. Yeah, so what you guys been up to?

Oh you know, the usual. Maria walked over to the stereo and turned the radio on. A hip-hop show was on, some bootleg 2Pac, and she turned it down a bit and sat back down. Just you know, doing stuff. I finished—she turned toward the window and stuck her head out. Hey, you watch what you're doing there buddy!

They all looked out the window. A neighbourhood drunk, a blond guy with a moustache, was on the ground. A guy in sunglasses and a black bomber jacket looked up at their window.

He's a racist. Are you a racist too?

Maria hesitated. No, but he's no threat to you. He doesn't know what he's saying. He's just out of it.

Jesus you know, that guy's always shooting his mouth off and saying stuff.

Yeah but usually the people around here don't take him seriously.

He's going to get into trouble, well, he probably already has.

Yeah, but did you see that time last Saturday? There was this big scene, and someone was yelling at him from their car, and this woman she like, was saying, what do you need, you know, doing the social-worker thing or the bible thing or something. And so she gives him a mirror, just pulls this mirror out of her bag and goes and gives it to him right there.

Oh yeah? No kidding.

Oh yeah, a real commotion. And I don't know, what's he going to do with a mirror?

Simon licked the joint to finish it and flicked a match. He took a couple of puffs and passed it to Candace.

Oh jeez, I don't know. Three on a match, eh?

Oh no, that only counts if you light 3 smokes with one match, like 3 separate cigarettes, eh?

Oh yeah, oh okay. Ha ha, oh, I don't know. Oh what the hay, eh?

May as well party.

Yeah really. You know Candace, I was telling Maria about there was this guy at work, and he's like this total asshole, and he's going on about stuff and just a real jerk.

Oh jeez, you know there's always these guys like that, you know they're like, let's get a beer after work. And you know, I've like known them for two days, and they're already just in your face, going on about how let's get together. Course usually they just take a couple wigs and that's it.

Maria took a drag. That's enough for me. Oh jeez Candace, we've just been smoking too much lately.

Oh yeah, it's getting tragic.

Assuming tragic proportions. Gonna have to stop.

We're going to go dry for awhile. Simon opened the hotel and dropped the roach in it. A week anyway.

Yeah, real heroes.

So, but what were you saying about that guy, Candace?

Hunh, what, the guy?

Yeah, the guy who just wanted 40 winks?

Hunh, oh, no, I said a couple of wigs. Don't you say that? Yeah we used to say that all the time, in the bar, you know, in the valley, they'd go have a couple wigs, eh? Yeah, c'mon, they'd go, have a couple wigs, you know, like swigs.

Oh yeah, that's hilarious. Maria took a sip of beer.

Hunh, pretty interesting. It's like when these people have their favourite sayings, and they're always going, whatever. Like there was this salesman I saw last week, and he's always going, bottom line. Or Let me be honest with you. Everyone's living these clichés.

Yeah well, you know, like it's a free country eh?

Oh yeah, I know, I'm just, I dunno.

Candace picked up the comics on the table. Hey, Snoopy, jesus, I haven't seen him in a long time.

Oh yeah, it's hilarious. D'you ever notice everything they say is with exclamation marks?

I think they get paid for that. They get paid more for anything that's not a period.

They do not. Who told you that?

I dunno. I just heard it somewhere, I read it somewhere.

No. It isn't true. Maria leaned back in her chair, laughing.

He drained his beer. Okay, well then remember, well this is probably before your time, but in the early '70s there was the *Donnie and Marie Show* and *Sonny and Cher.*

Yeah but later it was just *Cher.* Remember that? I remember the *Cher* show. She always had those great Bob Mackie dresses.

Oh yeah, weren't they great?

Yeah but remember the big backdrop she had too? Her name this big C? Yeah those were the days for variety shows, that's for sure. Bobby Vinton, you know, he had that song that goes "Moya really Krakatoa, means that I love you so," in Polish? I don't know, it goes something like that.

Yeah right. What's your point?

Okay, well, so like I was saying, there were these two shows. One of them *Donnie and Marie*—

The other one *Sonny and Cher*. Oh wow Simon, I don't know. That's pretty good. So this is all about some consipiracy or something?

No, it's just like I remember my sister saying to me, that she liked—

—wait, don't tell me, she liked *Sonny and Cher*?

No, she liked *Donny and Marie*.

Yeah, well, it figures. Didn't they do that song, "I'm not Lisa, my name is Julie?"

No, I think that, oh, maybe. I don't know.

But they did have that good song, "And They Called it Puppy Love."

Yeah, I think that was a Donny Osmond solo effort. I remember it in the fall, when I was going to Grade 5. Nineteen seventy-two I think. Our school didn't have a gym, so in the winter every Wednesday afternoon we went skating at the rink. It was really cold there too. I remember when I'd go to hockey practice Saturday mornings, if the janitor hadn't got there, and some kids put their skates on at home, so they didn't have to lace them up there—you know, the whole getting your skates tight enough thing—and these kids would be crying, it was colder inside than outside.

Oh you're crazy. Don't pay any attention to him, Candace. He's out of control. Enough, grandpa.

In my day, he squawked.

Maria stood up. You guys want some coffee? Candace, you want some coffee? I was going to make some. I'm bagged, I don't want to spend the whole weekend tired.

Oh sure, if you guys are having some. So hey Simon, did you guys go dancing in your snowmobile suits?

No, we had sock hops. I remember those, and rubbing my hand against some girl's velvet ass. I mean she was wearing velvet pants or something. That was my first sexual experience. About a year later I was laying on a toboggan and I felt something too. I had to beat this kid up, 'cause he was there with me.

Maria called out from the kitchen, wow you've progressed so far. At least we don't need a sled, no.

Hey, watch it! Yeah so Candace, what, d'you mean people used to wear their skidoo suits at dances?

Oh yeah, they still do, if someone has a wedding or whatever in the winter & they're going to some tavern. They just unzip their suits half way down, and they'll dance all night.

Crazy. Maria came back out from the kitchen. Well, I know that when my parents used to curl, I can remember sitting up in the caf, and the old guys'd be there, they didn't have a licence so they'd just have a mickey of rye and pour it into their coffee.

Yeah?

Yeah, but I guess they were still playing, or waiting for a rink, you know. Or it'd be a bonspiel, and they'd go down, and they'd be fucked up.

Hilarious.

Yeah well, I think once one guy cracked his knee. Or maybe that was the time my dad broke his leg. Or he had bursitis or something.

So you want to get going Maria? Oh no, you're making coffee.

Oh no, let's forget that. I've just got some water boiling. Let's go out. It's so beautiful out, I just want to go and sit in the park.

Hey yeah, you want to go on the swings?

Hunh, are you serious?

Oh yeah, he's serious. We'll see Simon. He's never going to get a job anyway, so he figured he may as well not grow up. »

«GENERALZ DIE IN PRIVATZ»

SHE CAME INTO their place and threw her stuff on a chair in the bedroom.

What're you reading?

Hunh? Oh, yeah, this. He showed it to her.

What's he wearing?

Uhh, I don't know. Some kind, I don't know, it says here a uh, a collier. Coal worker.

Oh yeah, they had some good pictures of them in that book I got from the library last week. In this book they said how, there was this thing and they were saying how people'd hand down their clothing from generations, and men would and people'd just buy used clothing from wherever and men would wear women's dresses and stuff.

Oh yeah, they were talking about that in here, about women working naked in the mines. Like on the one hand people'd be shocked at morals changing or—

Yeah and like now they're a woman can't do that. Fucken . . . .

Yeah well, you know. So how're you doing?

Not bad. You know. I'm going to have a bath.

Yeah, you feel like sparking one up first?

She could see him down the hallway, his nose in a book.

Yeah, okay, so like General Ludd.

The house around them was ridiculously small, they liked it. Crack dealers up the street, sagging sweat-pants, torn old ski jackets and, no, they were *down* the street, it's south. Not like, you know, *south* of Queen Street, Jones territory, or north, on College, magic realism, Lynn's goth divas. The dealers were like at the bottom of the street, just before the Ontario Housing. Little seams were shredded in their jackets. They were afraid of their dreams. Portuguese or Vietnamese pop from the restaurants at the top of the stairs, they were near a phone. All the phones in the area had to be tapped, there were video cameraz on the fences saying they were there to stop drug dealing or illegal activitiez but you still had to call 911 for an emergency. Did that mean they were dummies, like the ones you can buy in stores down on Adelaide, dummie video cameras for your fashion store? Or just people in the neighbourhood only count if they're criminalz, not if they're victims. Or something like that. They weren't like flashy, like in other parts of the city, they were downhome homebody homies. Fucken east coasters & shit. Kevin's loserz, selling to Gil walking thru the project, but not them, never Jimmy or Lucy. They'd joke about startin' a franchise, Maria & Simon's House of Crack. On other streets where it was more like heroin, a professor's kid blew the money his dad was going to spend on rehab. Different bugz lived at different times: or were popular. Lice then, & they had delousing stations, powder, cracking them in the seams of your heavy wool uniform. & now it was cockroaches, roach hotels, they called dealers roaches.

Yeah so I saw these things in the paper, you know about ludditism, & I think, so like one of them was saying about tech . . .

She mouthed, rolling her eyes. Oh wow. He thought of this girl sitting in a saucer of milk, licking it from her pussy. A book he read somewhere. He didn't have it anymore, traded it in for crack, I mean for CDs. Twenty good books, maybe three CDs. What the fuck.

I was getting some books together to bring up the street, and I guess I got this awhile ago and I never read it.

Yeah, well, it's big enough.

Yeah, I've got the time now. You know, when I brought them in I got a pretty good deal.

Why'd you use them to get CDs, you could've used the money?

Well, you know, I didn't.

[*in the store*]

We've got some new stock. Well, most of them were yours.

Yeah, it's a slippery slope you know, bringing in books to trade for CDs. Next it's CDs for crack, then I'll have to go down & sell my blood.

Yeah, so, whatever. She was moving around in her top.

What the fuck, can you see if there's something in the back there, twisting it around.

Yeah, no. He got up and ran his fingers in the back seam of her thermal top. No. Nada.

Fuck man! Drives me crazy. I thought I could, you know, feel something there. It's like these things. She was pulling at it.

He pointed at the little bow on her top. Yeah, so why do they have them there at the front?

I don't know the—to tell you you're a girl? I'dunno. He put his fingers on the sides of her rib cage and his thumbs ran down the front of her tits, flicking a bit at her nipples.

Hey, watch it there fella.

Hosebag. Hey, you feel good.

Yeah, well look who's talking eh?

Guitars were banging away on the stereo. She raised her hand in the two-fingered salute. Fock! Right on!

Yeah, it's hilarious. I really like these guys.

Yeah, they're okay. Even if it is a bit like the Black Crowes.

No way, I don't know, maybe get their letters scratched on my arm.

Don't be an idiot. Oh, do whatever you want.

Well, I'dunno. I might. No, I think I want to get a, you know, one of those big native ones, maybe on my back.

She was sitting on his lap, and he kissed her on the side of her neck. He ran his hand over her cut-offs. Yugo'sbmps.

Hunh? What's that sailor?

I said you got goosebumps.

She lifted up her ass. Oh hey, sorry, didn't mean to—

He reached into his pantz & adjusted his hard-on. »

«UNDO MOMMY»

AFTER AWHILE, HE GOT QUIET. Jessica walked behind the man who spoke bad Vietnamese. The night was damp and cold. Worms the size of twigs extended from the grass onto the sidewalk so she walked carefully. She wore a sweatshirt that said Sea Semester at Sea. It was one of those seconds, she got it at the flea market in the old Safeway at Knight and King Edward.

He turned up a sidewalk going along a rotting fence. The yard was full of sticks strung together with plastic produce bags flapping in the foggy wind. It started raining and she saw drops silver-flecked in the streetlight. He bent down and opened his briefcase. Then he stood up and unlocked the door at the side of the house.

The room was hot, humid. A beefy guy with a crew-cut sat on a huge couch in his boxers and shirt and tie. He looked at her and then back at the TV.

The missionary she came in with told her to take a seat. He walked through the room asking if she wanted something to drink.

She said okay, expecting a light beer.

He came back in with a bottle of Jack Daniels, two glasses and a six-pack. Ok man let's kick it. Thinking, two each, have a shot and chug the first and get a good buzz going. Fast.

Jessica noticed the missionary on the couch had his hand down his boxers, trying to dislodge something from between his balls and his anus. He looked at her and finished the job quickly.

Hey, Bob, move it hunh. Her guy sat down on the couch.

It's Bill.

Yeah, whatever.

She didn't know his real name. She met him on the bus, when she heard him speaking to an old lady. He was talking Vietnamese, but badly, or so it seemed to her. His badge said Mr. Nguyen and his church in Vietnamese.

When he was growing up everyone he knew was in the church youth group. All his friends—they'd hang out at the church, go to bible discussion youth groups led by an earnest, balding, aircraft mechanic. They'd sing songs, and at summer camp they'd make out, sneak out and party and spend the rest of the time in the sulfurous trees, firing off rounds at the range, chewing targets into thin lace doilies.

She was glad she got her homework done. She'd done a paper on anorexia, anoresia. A lot of girls had it. She didn't. She sat with two Latter-Day Saints watching a TV show about pueblo churches in Mexico. She wasn't sure if it was Mexico. But it looked nice and hot and bright. »

«SAY AGAIN NOT REPEAT»

WHEN I GOT to the laundromat the kid of the Korean guy had *This Week in Baseball* playing on the TV. I threw my stuff in and went next door for a coffee. Some guys from the job site across the street were in there. I poured myself a coffee and got in line between the two of them and the guy with the paper and coffee said he'd pay for the other guy's stuff. He had a bag of chips and a big Dr. Pepper.

That's pretty good he's buying you breakfast, I said to the lucky guy. I was wearing my good belt.

Yeah, look, he's not going to be able to afford it. He doesn't have the money. The guy behind the counter was doing it up on the machine and the total came to $8.38. The guy pulled out a ten.

Money left from the weekend the other guy said. He picked up a bottle of something from next to the licorice twizzlers box on the counter.

What the fuck's this?

There were little balls like styrofoam packing material, but real small, in the bottle. It looked like a little lava lamp.

Jesus, looks pretty bad eh?

That's fucking crap! he yelled. He shoved it back and said to the grinning store guy. Sorry, guess that's not good marketing eh?

Later that day I went to visit my grandmother. The crack house next to her had a couple bmx bikes on its front lawn. Walking in from the bus stop I could smell coffee from the church or maybe from Church's Chicken. A fresh steaming stream of piss ran from a corner in the alley, the foam at its front the shape of a aspirin caplet.

Grandma was wearing her yellow track suit, with drawstrings at her bosom thick as her arthritic knuckles. She pulled me inside. The guy on the radio she had blasting said this was Clifford Olson country, and then he said it was a bungle in the jungle, not in Canada. Those white wine drinkers got what they deserved. My grandma served me a rye and water and I had a couple donuts as well. We talked about my cousin who was home-schooling her kids 'cause they talked back at the elementary school.

After, I helped Grandma do the dishes. Placing the Corelle carefully on the thin foam she had on the counter next to the sink, a packing material sheet with the give of a panty liner.

At the laundromat when I got back with my coffee, the kid and the guy who was in there reading a Louis Lamour with his walkman on were watching the gymcercize show, the girls on it bending over at the waist and cooing at the camera.

I got home from my grandma's after dark, and the magnolia she'd given me had dried in my lapel to the colour of a ripped-off condom. »

«THE PET DETECTIVE»

I'M LOOKING AT THE RECORD I'm rolling up on, it's that Poison one with his tongue out and he's totally made up. Guys rock when they—okay sure, let's get groovy. The dirty coffee line on the edge of the paper, from my saliva I guess, just beer. Kenny wanted like *Boyz in the Hood* being 6 and I got the original *Scream* to veg out to later. Forgot, *Samuellll* Jackson, so cool to cop the dad, little organ gangbangers. Kenny falls asleep ten minutes in, leaning back on my knees; I gotta wait till like Act One from the barricaded fat kids, back as Ice-T or Ice-Cube. Then it's pop 'im off to bed but I step on one of his McD's toys in the middle of the floor in the middle of my foot. Fuckin' cheap plastic kills, I scream, Ironic, eh? but Kenny's out cold. Lucky for me. He's in bed soon, finish the joint as *Boyz* rewinds for its return and *Scream*'s up, that suddenly she's really stabbed & it's not ironic anymore—the phone rings. Deb's Al drove around all day with her BC Benefits cheque, he wants to know if she's over.

Al use' to hang out with the dealer & jailbait downstairs & Deb'd come over skulking on the lawn or sitting next to the kiddylitterbox, ear to nude drywall. Onea my ex's started calling her Double Oh 7. Say, hey Double Oh 7 howzitgoin'? Al phones again, asks if she's there again, I say no again, hang up again.

Al phones again again, asks if she's there again again, I say no again again, hang up again again. Al phones again again again, asks if she's there again again again, I say no again again again, hang up again again again. He calls back a sec later. If I see her ask her to call him, okay—he said that. And said it again, and said it again again, and said it again again again.

I'm confused by the movie, getting up to answer the phone too often. Al doesn't have a cell so it's no tracing problem, he's actually there where he says he is, at home. By the time it shows up in the movies you can already do something against it. Fingerprints. Star 69.

DNA from her cunt, like that lady down east what's her name?

Al phones to ask if Deb's around. Everytime he calls I'm patient and say no, listen slow and patient to his whining. I unplug the machine and phone. Then the not noise is unnerving as the movie winds up. There's too many lights on in their house on the video and not enough here in mine. Neither seems to protect. The phone answers I put on someone else's voice, say don't call back, he asks who it is.

In the morning their kids knock on the door downstairs. I push Kenny away from me, down to check it out. Pushing. He phones at 8:30. Scored a cellphone somewhere. Lucky it's a Saturday, fuck off. Kenny's chin jam dribble sticks apple juice to my elbow guy on the radio is on about fishing. I go outside and part of a skin-thread raccoon's still plastered to the top of the front right tire on Deb's pick-up. Deb and Al's kids Sonny and Felena play with a gameboy without earphones in the truck bed as Al snores.

If I close my eyes, is Kenny there? The video store, cold beer and wine store, cardboard cutouts of scenes from a movie commercial tie-in African safari drink he wants. The display's missing a leg. A beach, big logs up for sitting, not arranged like in Vancouver, but natural. Kenny tests his diaper in a tidal pool. The magazine Deb brought over late last night has pictures of a guy. Streaks a beach, hand damaged from wood versus japanese swords. Al said sure, go over with your indian friends. Guys who fuck good aren't good for much else unless.

On Monday, at work, Mary's lifestyle hints go by useless without. I can sort of get it done in time. They're going to have it system-wide but my contract'll be up by then without. Her cell goes at lunch. Deb's mom looking for me. The sound's crappy so I can't hardly hear her moaning. Maybe Deb, quick, oh no.

Guess she got Mary's cell number from work when she phoned there. Al hadn't worked for a couple months now. He was contributing. The thing was when he worked, Deb said, you don't know what it's like—I can't. I ask Mary can I take along her cell, tho fuck knows a grey brick in black perforated vinyl, like cheese with a white pencil in it, is hardly fashionable. My favourite old Big Blue jacket's got no pockets in case I have to call someone. Drive my little shitbox past the daycare of Kenny. At Deb and Al's house 2 or 3 cop cars, ambulance, firetruck—they always get there first.

Cop looks at me like an older sister he hasn't seen for good reason for ten years. I get past him and go in, but stop with the quiet of the TV-still, a commercial soundtrack you forget, you've seen the commercial so many times now. Without having ever seen white thighs and muddy murky insides.

Deb's mom's outside having a smoke at the picnic table. She's as grey as that Honda I traded in. Deb's on the floor in the living room I just walked out of, looking like she's stretching her back by leaning over the coffee table. Sonny about to get up and check if there's any food in the fridge, in cut-offs and tartan slippers. They said Felena was upstairs being bagged in her and Sonny's bedroom.

Deb's mom's cousin got the contract to be grief counsellor part-time at the school and part-time anyone else. But she had to put down she was non-related so her getting the contract wasn't in the paper. Al was going to go to the States. He was going to come back and get his tools the next day but they arrested him at the motel where he was staying. Deb's truck was parked at the mall lot until it was single. There was an article in the paper on what she did wrong. You can protect yourself. This lady who did the article stayed at the Coastal Inn, but the photographer who took my picture didn't like the Coastal and stayed at the bed and breakfast on the highway. He was gay. It was that place where they have a carved driftwood sign, gravel driveway and a nice carport.

I helped Al get the work at our place. He did a good job painting and the drywall where the stairs doorway to downstairs used to be, but he didn't finish. »

three

«MISCARRIAGE COLLECTION»

SO D'YOU WANT ANYTHING? Some coffee?

No, got a coffee on my way over. Wouldn't mind a beer, but not before noon, that's one of the AA questions, Do you drink before noon? No.

Oh yeah, I've got friends they're like, is it quarter to? Close enough?

Jane jumped around her sister's living room, acting out her latest ex-boyfriend. So I didn't tell you about the fair eh? Oh man, it was hilarious. Yeah, so you know I haven't seen Bert since then eh? I don't know, he's uh, he's something. You know, like we went to the bar, like this time we went to the bar and Yvonne's taking care of Jess, right, so I can relax, I don't have to get up in the morning, and he always wants to go. *I don't like this bar, there's bikers here, they don't like how I dance.* You know, cause he's kind of feminine. But you know that time I went over to Van and he—oh man I feel so shitty for borrowin' that money from Sam to get back, you know. 'Cause Bert's like let's go over & visit them right and I go I can't, I'm broke, you know. And he's like don't worry about it.

She did it in a deeper voice for Bert.

Don't worry about it! She pushed away something, like she was wiping an invisible table. So I'm whatever, you know, sure. And then on the ferry goin' over he's, don't you think it's only fair if we split it? You know, like the ferry fare? And what? I'm like What? WHAT? It's just like him I got so pissed off, I knew I'd have to get some money from Sam. So I just said that, you know. It's just like that time we went to this wedding. His cousin's wedding? In Ladysmith? He asks me, you know, you want to go with me to this wedding. And I go, you know, I can't afford a babysitter, going to a wedding, I don't know if the booze is free and I can't afford it if it's not. And so he goes I'll take care of it, you know, the babysitting, and then when the time comes he goes, Jane don't you think we should split it. Don't you think it's fair? I mean yeah, like it's fair, if only I'd known about it I wouldn't've gone in the first place, right? But the wedding was pretty funny though. So, you know, did I tell you about his dad?

No. Shelley watched her kid pull her dress over her head. Jane's boy was crayonning a Fisher-Price toy. They're high quality, but she didn't say anything.

Oh yeah, about when Bert and his dad're trying to kill each other? It was after the wedding. But you know, we get there, and we stopped at this pub in town before we got there, had a couple beers, some highballs, smoked a joint, you know, just to get ready. And I get there and I'm sitting in the church next to, I don't know, some guy I didn't see later and I'm like whoah 'cause I'm a bit loaded. But what I didn't know was like they're all Bluenosers, from Nova Scotia, right, so everyone was hammered before the wedding even started, the bride & groom, probably the minister for all I know. And like Bert's dad, he's old but he's got this girlfriend, she was hardcore. You know, she's travelled all around, she's maybe forty, forty-five—she's in good shape, I'll give her that—no grey hair. And she just latches right on to me at the reception, right? I'm like I guess everyone was watching us going oh, Mary's got Jane now, she's got her in her clutches. But you know, we just partied right. And then after.

So, what, did you drive back here all the way?

Oh no, we were stayin' at some other cousin's place eh? And her daughter looked after Jess and I checked in on him when we got back, he was fine. And so we go back there, it's I don't know, 2:00, 3:00, and I have a beer, but then I'm ready to crash, right? You know, it's been good, I've put in a shift, right?

Yeah right.

You know, but Bert keeps pounding, and his dad is, and as for Mary, jesus, you've never seen someone drink like that. And then she goes, or something, and Bert starts massaging her neck.

She acted it out with dramatic hand gestures, like she was kneading dough, her fingers splayed and stiff then loose. He's like, ooh, all you know, gross, and his dad's like just as long as he doesn't get a woodie. You know, it's fine, as long as he doesn't get a woodie.

Oh no, that's hilarious.

Oh yeah, isn't it? Fuck, you know, as long as he's not enjoying it too much. And I'm like whatever, I don't care, you know, I'm about to pass out. But then

Bert moves his hands down her shoulders or whatever, I don't know, and then his dad jumps him, and they're all over the floor, rolling around. Jane dropped onto her back on the floor, and Shelley's daughter started crying. Jane straightened up. What's that, oh, sorry baby, sorry Caroline, don't you worry, auntie's just playing. Yeah so anyway, they're goin' at it, and the VCR goes flying, beers, ashtrays and then like Bert just gets up and takes off outside. And then Jess is crying from the next room so I go in there. 'Cause like when he starts crying I'm just like sober, right. Right away. So I go in there, and he's all upset, it's a strange room, noise from the living room where everyone's yelling. And I'm just standing there, holding her, walking around. Jesse sat on the floor as his mom walked back and forth, telling her story. And you know, Bert's dad was pretty pissed, he was all embarrassed, 'cause Bert had him around pretty soon.

Oh yeah? He got him on his back?

Yeah 'cause like his dad jumped him right, right onto him when he was still rubbing Mary, but Bert had him down on his back pretty soon, and he was I'm going to kill you, I could kill you right now. She did her deep Bert voice again, shaking her cupped hands. I'm gonna kill you! He was just doing it. And so his dad was, you know. But then I'm in there with Jess and suddenly he just slams open the door, Bert, and he's like I was outside there and where are you? You don't care about me at all. Where are you? And then he just leaves. He didn't even see me, I was just standing there, holding Jess and he didn't even see me. I'm just like this, right? And Jess was just getting calmed down, and I couldn't do anything with him then, so I just had to lie down with him and I didn't get to sleep until, I don't know, 4:30.

Oh killer.

Yeah no kidding right? 'Cause I guess Bert slept in his car, and then he came banging on the door to get into the house at 7:30, so I get maybe 3 or 4 hours of sleep. I was dead.

» » »

He walked toward her, putting his hands around her neck. Let me just massage you, relax you, his grip tightening.

He talked about his mother being dead, the bitch, his feelings for his sister.

In Ontario, the farmers have accents that waver between Cockney, Yorkshire, Scottish. I don't know those accents very well, so maybe that's an inaccurate statement.

He and his sister were trying to kill his mental wife.

His sister wasn't really dead.

Everyone laughed when the guy said he missed his departed wife—the bitch. He said she was suited for farm life because she was a cow and some people laughed at that.

It was very realistic.

His sister had long hair, lots of hairspray, lots of eye make-up and she'd done some commercials and a Christian rock video.

She was upset because she didn't have any make-up for the weekend. He had a nervous breakdown and threw up but he was ready half an hour later.

His girlfriend asked if he put his hand on her breast and we said they were practically undressed and they had their tongues down each other's throats. But we were joking.

He was working on his thesis. He only got married for the money, the scholarships, the research proposals.

Everyone was happy to see him up there.

It was a legion so he had to take his hat off, even though he had dandruff.

Oh yeah, so your brother's a psycho eh?

It was like Paul Bernardo but with a tragic ending.

» » »

Ian looked at the card Shelley'd given him.

Oh you're not getting that out are you? Tom looked up from the joint he'd rolled.

Yeah, I just thought they might like to see it.

What is it? Paul looked over his boyfriend Ian's shoulder. There were two sets of baby footprints on the outside, one right-side up and the other upside down. He couldn't make out the words, the room was dark.

Shelley came back from the kitchen. She put a tray of nachos on the coffee table among the bowls of dip, ash-trays, glasses, candles, *TV Times*, *Pennysaver*, remote, and junk.

Hey Shel those look great. So let's check the weather. Jane reached over for the remote.

No it doesn't work, Tom said. Here. He got up and

walked over to the TV. The screen lit up, brightening the room, and he kept pushing a button, the channels flicking by until he flew by the weather channel. He turned it back. When're you headin' over?

Oh, 'bout 9. Maybe get the 9.

Yeah so, he read the text at the bottom of the screen. Supposed to be a good crossing. Lookit the water, a bit choppy, no whitecaps.

Yeah really. Okay, thanks Tom. So what's the card you guys got over there?

It's—we got it from these friends of ours, Shelley said. They keep having miscarriages, she does, and the last time it was twins, and they sent out this card.

Oh no.

Ian finished looking at it and put it on the armrest, looking at the knee holes in his jeans. Paul picked it up. Wow, this is heavy.

Oh yeah eh?

Yeah, we've got this friend of ours, right? Ian?

Oh you mean Henry.

Yeah, Henry. He comes from a really fucked up family. Well, I guess we all do. You know, dysfunction-al.

What do you mean, Tom asked, dysfunctional?

Oh you know, people can't talk to each other. And 'specially 'cause he's a homo, so.

Yeah but doesn't that mean to imply that there's a functional family?

Listen Tom dear, let me put it this way. Poor people are dysfunctional. Rich people aren't. That's why most homo's are rich, they come from rich families.

That doesn't make sense, I don't get it.

Okay. Most people—most straight people—think to be a fag you have to come from some fucked up family. That's a myth. It's not true. Actually, most homo's come from rich families or ones that give them enough security to explore their love in a dysfunctional society. It's society that's dysfunctional. And dysfunctional families don't produce fags, they produce serial killers and rapists. No offence. Some of them may be gay, but most aren't, just like normal people.

Tom laughed.

Paul said, it's true. No one's going to be gay if they're worried about self-esteem. And as a rule, people from dysfunctional families lack self-esteem. But don't worry dear, he patted Tom's imaginary hand. There's different kinds of dysfunctional, right?

Tom got back into the argument with his big point.

But if there aren't any functional families, then how can there be dysfunctional ones? You said so yourself.

Tom just 'cause there's different ways families get fucked up doesn't mean you can't say they're fucked up.

Yeah so, Ian continued, tell them about Henry's stepmother.

Oh yeah, Paul goes. Henry's this old friend of mine. After his dad got remarried I went to their new place, out in New West, and it was his stepmom's house for years, and she'd never had any kids, but she had 4 or 5 miscarriages.

Tom thought of a woman he'd once dated, who kept trying to have babies with whatever guy she slept with, never used birth control, and kept having miscarriages, and going to the hospital with her and meeting her parents, them thinking it was his miscarriage this time but they'd never fucked, she didn't understand why he didn't want to. They lost touch, and he kept the story to himself.

And for each one she had this ceramic doll on a shelf. She had a lot of stuff, spoons in a rack, regular stuff, you know, Blue Mountain, little crystal animals, and I guess she had this miscarriage collection or something, that was her way of dealing with it, like these ceramic dolls she got at the gift shop at the Bay or Zellers.

» » »

Later, on the ferry back to the mainland, they walked by a man with long, lank grey-white hair, muttering about writing the great Canadian hockey novel, scribbling on a sheet of printed words. Children's naked weiners poked obscenely out of cardboard boats in the cafeteria. Teenagers roamed aimlessly and with purpose, and smokers huddled on the decks, sucking the second-hand smoke back into their blissing lungs.

They came back inside and sat down next to a couple with a baby, the carseat on the floor. The baby eyed his tea and his parents talked about Don, the update they got from Lisa. Two of his arteries ruptured near the heart, and so they decided he had to be moved to Victoria. They didn't take him by air ambulance because they didn't think it was too serious, just needed moving. So they phoned all his boys, and they went down. And by the time he got to Victoria he was in a coma. The case was handled really badly. He had enough presence of mind to get his family together in the room.

And later, it became a question of how long it'd take you to get back in shape. She still had a month to go to get fit. It'd been five months. Sometimes people just let themselves go. That one woman, the friend of theirs, he didn't want to say anything against her but she just didn't try after she had the baby. Whereas the other woman, she worked out for an hour every day for nine months until she had the baby and then she was back in a month. And so if you don't do anything, if you haven't exercised in a year, it's going to take 4 or 5 months to get back in shape. Or maybe 6 months, so she still had a month. »

«CHRISTIAN RODEO»

I KNEW DONALD DRANSFIELD and George Filgate for maybe seven years in the 1970s. At 14, Dransfield had the awkward, loping gait of someone growing in spastic spurts. George was smaller, darker. Dransfield had red hair, George's was black, both of them greased it back and wore Wrangler or GWG jeans, bucket cuffs over scuffed shoes or boots, a pre-designer dark blue, hands in their back pockets and gravel kicked around.

We all went to bible camp a couple summers in a row, or maybe the spring when the snow hadn't melted from the central Alberta prairie and highway. We played complicated scripture scavenger hunts with bored staff members, went shooting with .22s and riding muscular horses that knew the country like a 7-11 parking lot.

» » »

Dransfield phoned me up on a Friday night just as I was trying to freepour 7-Crown rye into a little apple-juice bottle.

Maria asked me how it was going.

Wouldn't be so hard if you hadn't put that last mickey in the bluebox.

Well I didn't know. It's for you, it's Don.

I got it and asked him what's up.

I need a big favour.

Sure what is it.

Are you busy tomorrow afternoon?

Uh, no, don't think so.

Can you help me go pick up a fridge?

He'd asked me to help him a couple weeks ago. I said to him, You found one.

Yeah.

Sure, where is it?

Out in Point Grey. Dunbar.

Okay sure, when?

He told me he was going to a tool rental place to get a fridge dolly and I said I'd pick him up there. We agreed on 1:30.

When I got to the tool rental place I told them my buddy was coming down & I was meeting him there. Then he came in and we got the dolly. Don left a cash deposit of 60 bucks.

We drove across town to a pretty ordinary looking big place next to a mini-forest. A yellow Baycrest fridge sat in the carport and a woman about our age came down the stairs from the deck.

I was looking for the receipts because we had some work done on it but we've been so busy and it wasn't in the renovation file. She passed the owner's booklet to Don and he thanked her and stuck it in the freezer. But it's fine. We want to get a summer cottage and then maybe we'd use it, but we did the renovation and—she smiled—it isn't white! Don said it looked great and she said we've only lived here about ten years. Boy the job I had with it, they had kids and there were stickers all over it! You know I was working at the top of my field then, the top of my career, but I just wasn't feeling right? And I was in California and I went to this teacher who teaches life skills using myth, and there was this one time, when he said something that really stuck with me. He would sit in the centre of all of us, on pillows, with his books, but he never opened them, because, you know, he was basically telling us stories. He would talk about how important it was to answer the call and go on a journey, your adventure, and if you didn't you'd keep hearing the call afterwards like a song you remember. And one time at lunch break—he would always eat lunch with his students—I asked him about the call, because I was feeling dissatisfied, and I didn't know if I was doing what I was supposed to be doing. And he told me this story about a Swiss psychologist, who was feeling low in energy and he looked back at his childhood, you know, because you have all this energy then. And he remembered that he used to like building little stone houses when he was a child. So he built himself a stone house by a lake, and he actually was physically involved in it, and he got his energy back.

» » »

We drove around a bit looking for somewhere to eat on our way back to Dransfield's. He was more hungover than me, and we ended up at a Mexican place in Kits.

Some figure skating was on and I half-watched it while he fretted about the fridge. I'd parked the truck around the corner.

D'you think it's okay?

I dunno. Maybe. It's a big B&E neighbourhood tho. I was giving him the gears.

Oh I'm gonna go check.

I smiled at him and had another swallow of Kokanee. After a couple of minutes he hadn't come back and I headed outside, leaving my bomber on my seat to hold our table. Going around the corner I saw Don on the bed of the pickup, leaning back against the cab window, a little guy with scaling skin choking him and trying to get his knee into Don's crotch. A guy across the street was yelling at the guy to let go of Don and the fridge was leaning off the open tailgate onto a souped up white Honda parked behind me, the paint still new enough that it didn't crack in the fiberglass dent. I pulled the guy off and the samaritan across the street came over to join in. We kicked the thief a bit and then someone said the cops were coming. Don and I heaved the fridge back onto the truck and took off.

We pulled over a couple of blocks away on a leafy sidestreet busy with "Save the CBC" signs. We shared a smoke and let the shakes die down. I tasted the beer in my mouth again and remembered my jacket back at the pub.

I gotta go back.

Hunh? What for?

I left my jacket at the table.

Oh fuck, well what did you do that for?

Listen, who cares. It's my leather so I'm gonna go back and get it. As it is this is the first time I've worn it in over a month.

How come?

'Cause Maria gave it to some guy as collateral for money she owed him.

Oh shit.

Yeah, I told her, why don't you get a life and leave me? It's pathetic, you know? She's crazy. The other day I thought she'd puked out the kitchen window, but she'd just scraped the stuff out of a samosa.

Serious.

We parked a block from the restaurant and I went in and paid for the beer and left with my jacket. »

«FRENCH CANADIAN UNITS»

THE THING IS, what everyone knew was, if you talk to a buddya mine who was over there, you know, he'll, he'll tell ya, you know, he'll tell ya, ya, you know he'll tell ya, it'd get much worse. If they found the stuff, the documents about what happened, what really happened, it'd sure be a lot worse. But, you know, it's the higher-ups. I mean, if you go to everyone above colonel, you know, they don't know what the heck's going on.

I think they know what's going on. Oh sure.

No 'cause if they, my—we've got a really . . . our unit you know, here we've got a really good colonel you know, our base commander's . . . but you know, there hasn't been a good general since Lewis MacKenzie.

Oh, I don't know. I don't think you can.

You know, everyone since then. I've been in for 10 years and I can tell you.

When we, when we went, when we went—I don't know—but I'm sure you know the guys over there, they were just soldiers doing a soldier's job. You know it's not a job to . . . it's not a job to give a soldier . . . but the thing is there's no one but a solider to give it to.

Yeah, well, that's a good way to put it. 'Cause you know, if they're saying he's not a team-player, he's got a family now . . . and besides, maybe he should try some more to be a team-player. 'Cause he's got a real problem with authority.

Yeah, well it fucked him up in the military didn't it?

Yeah, 'cause you know, now I don't want to wear my uniform in the mall. I don't want anyone to know. And I know my mom, when I joined she was real proud, you know, because before I had the long hair and that. But now she's not.

You know when he was there putting his hand on the flag, to take the oath, and then when he got out he was different. I don't want to say, well he's okay now, but he sat me down and explained his code of ethics to me and I just think people don't want that anymore.

They're tired of it, they're sick of wars and the killing, they just want it to stop.

And you know, like morale, you know . . . we haven't had a raise in five years but no one's complaining, we're just doing our job. You know, it's not a good job but we're not complaining, we're just doing it. We're just doing our job, you know. I mean, we're overseas now, and you know, there's guys who'll tell you anything you want to know about it. An' privates only make twelve thousand a year for the first four years, but you won't hear any complaining, 'cause you know, we're not proud but we're doing our jobs. And about that hazing, you know what no one's saying, is that it's all French Canadian units, you know, doing it, none of the English, you know, Canadian units. »

«BAD RELIGION OR FUGAZI»

THE THING ABOUT cops here, RCMP here, BC cops, they're more laid back. Like if they pull you over they'll just give you a warning, you know, just don't let me catch you again. But in Alberta, man, they're psycho.

Man, that'd be the worst thing, man. The back-door search. Spread the cheeks, here it comes. Oh man I can almost feel it.

Fuck, I thought it was gonna happen to me.

'Cause, one time we were coming back from Winnipeg, eh? So we had half an ounce for the road and we got pulled over.

There was this roach in the ashtray. I was too baked to notice it. And he kept sayin' I know you've got some.

But I had it tucked way up here eh, sliding his hand in the air over his head, in the, that visor thing.

Fuck when my step-dad killed my dog I was wrecked. And he was like, you're going to school tomorrow and I'm like I'm not! »

«YOU CAN'T BEAT RURAL WOMEN»

I WALKED TO THE EDGE of the rocks and watched a dozen sea lions watch me. They floated in the water, diving down, then reappearing, so it was difficult to count them. They just hung there, 30-40 feet off shore, looking at me, some of them looking at me and each other. Another pack came up, honking like a police cruiser on a frozen night.

My fingers were numb and I thought about rolling a joint & hotboxing it back in the truck. »

«CLASSIC»

OH YEAH, he turned out to be a real psycho eh? Had to call the cops and everything. First he wants to buy me an operation for my boobs then he's calling me a cunt and a bitch and a slut. Yeah, you remember I got him to co-sign that loan for me, to go back to school? Yeah, he's like, well soon as you got that money you soon reverted to your sluttish ways. And he'd call me and leave all these horrible messages on my machine and then he'd call back and go oh, Jane, I love you. Fuck! And then he came up to see me and I didn't know he was coming? And I was going out with someone and he called me up and said I was just a slut and a bitch. Oh yeah, really abusive. A good thing we didn't stay together, he probably would've turned out to be physically abusive too. 'Cause you never know. And you know, then Frieda's stepmom is like, try and keep this one. She doesn't know! You don't know until you're under the same roof. I just feel they should stop judging me, you know?

His girlfriend was up the street, doing her laundry. It was that magic hour, 7 to 8, *Wheel of Fortune* and *Jeopardy*. Vanna, the goddess of the trailer park, was being taunted by Pat about her dress. How long can you hold your arms up. He asked her what kind of art she liked. Oh, everything from contemporary art to the Old Master, she answered. Me, Pat goes, I like nothing better than when I get home to put my feet up and look at a painting of dogs playing poker.

When I got to Eaton's the girls at the perfume counter were trying to spritz everyone with some perfume. The name of it was written on their T-shirts. Maria stopped at the cK One counter and shot some behind her ears. On the escalator we heard a booming male voice. Miss Taylor, you've certainly been a target of the sleazy tabloid press with regard to your love life. Would you care to comment on that? Well, you put it right when you said "sleazy."

I was wondering if it was just the radio when we

came up to the fourth floor and there was Liz sitting on the stage over in the corner, with everyone standing around her. We stayed at Debbie Reynolds' hotel when we were in Vegas last week. She was married to Eddie Fisher when he left her for Liz, but if someone left me like that I wouldn't want them back. One time she was out on the street because of his gambling debts, and she was ten million dollars in debt. Someone asked Liz what kind of music she liked, new country or classic rock and she said that she liked rock and classical. »

«KILL WHITEY»

A COUPLE OF YEARS AGO I'd a been impressed by some chick who was supposed to be fucking her brother but these day's if you haven't slept with some younger male relative I don't even want to know you, know what I'm saying? Maria's coffee came out her nose as she chuckled at Josie's diatribe. I said don't mind us, I just gotta get a bigger screwdriver.

Anything I can help with sweetie? The crotch of Marie's sweatpants was patched a couple crazy times, a quilt that wouldn't quit colouring. The screwcap from the Bailey's had fallen under the chesterfield and I saw it as I walked into the kitchen and then when I came back out I reached down and picked it up and ran my tongue round its furry sharp edge before putting it back on the barracks box coffeetable. Naw, we don't need an expert.

We're back at the car tryin' to loosen the screws on the plate holder. Pete was scuffing the soggy leaves with his frayed shoe toe. What I don't get is how come they can't pick you up from a new plate?

I'd had to explain this to him a million times, but I'm nothing if not patient. Look, they've got this CPIC thing, right? The Canadian p'lice computer. The cops can run your plate or your drivers into it & they know everything about you, right? So first of all, what you do is you take your keys or whatever—I took the blunt edge of my three-foot driver—and you fuck up the bar code and shit on the back. Pete had one of those new licenses with his picture permanently embedded in it, a credit card kind of thing. So that means they can't run it through, right? It slows the pigs down.

Yeah, so they key in your number. Then they know I've got these priors, right?

No, if they key in the number, all they get is Highway stuff. That's why you wipe some goober or whatever, something good and sticky, right here. I pointed at the dark photo of him. So then they take it from you and that's where he puts his finger, right? His thumb or whatever, right?

Oh I get it. He stamped his feet. Man, it's as cold here as it was in Hawaii.

Yeah. Fuck. I'm back at the plate now and it won't come off. I pulled it back, popping the plastic threads at the back and landing on my ass. Fuck. Look, fuck this, let's go back inside, grab another beer. It was starting to rain anyhow, so we get inside and Josee starts telling us about her praise jesus relatives.

Yeah, so they're like total thumpers right? »

«A ELECTRIC FRYING PAN»

SIMON OPENED THE CUPBOARD. I was sitting on a kitchen chair next to a stack of cardboard boxes in the front of his house on a sunny winter morning.

Jane, you seen this?

He pulled out a frying pan, a electric one. I slurped some tea. "Beercan" was playing on the telephone-clock radio I got him last year for Christmas. Is that mom's?

Yeah. Cool eh?

She's been dead five years so it's kind of cool when you think about it. Kind of sick too, though.

Jeez Christmas is so different now eh? Remember when we were kids and we always wanted to open the big present first? We couldn't wait.

» » »

Jane was on the bus with her younger brother Jake.

Jake was excited to be going downtown. He was going to trade his half a green garbage bag of cans for 5¢ each at a place on Hastings. Afterwards he'd wander the bright lights, neon, slick sweet hopeful junkies' faces, buildings a warm small city's luxury of soapstone sandstone front façade.

Jake grinned glumly.

Hey, you know, there's places down here where moms take their clothes off? Jason saw it, he went in a bar here. He pointed at The Cobalt. And then this big bouncer came. Jake's voice quavered. Chased him out, bam!

Jane looked out the bus window. Man, your cans sure smell.

Yeah, well, at least I'll be able to buy something.

I don't need to. My boyfriend'll get it for me. So Vic's gonna get a job hey.

Yeah, well, what if you ate all their ex-lax—

She grimaced. What're you talking about?

—and you shit out this giant turd and you had seven inches on your asshole that had to be stitched up?

Hey, I'd just call him up, Vic, c'mon. She laughed.

Oooh, wouldn't want to lick that.

Yeah, right.

Hey, I did my talk today at school.

Oh yeah? No kidding. What'd you talk about stupid? She was pretty.

Flat tops.

Flat tops! What, like boobs?

No! He giggled. Aircraft carriers fuckin' bitch-ho skan—

Hey, fuck off! She said it like she meant it. Did you have fun?

Yeah.

Who's your girlfriend?

Hunh?

You know, know what I mean? Who d'you love? Tina?

No, she's flat as a piece of paper.

Yeah? Who then?

I dunno.

Get their picture. She laughed. Tell them your sister has to see it first.

The bus pulled up to Hastings and Main. Guys on the sidewalk called out their wares in a street poetry of freebase rock, pot, ups, downs. She bounced on her toes waiting for the bus door to open. They poked each other.

D'you wanna go to Simon's later?

No, I'm just going to hang out down here.

It's his new place.

Yeah, I know. »

«TOP 10 SCREW-UPS IN THE O.J. SIMPSON DEFENCE JOKE»

I LIKE TO LET my gut hang out over my boxers. When I have a hard-on I'll stand in the bathroom, a fork stuck under an apple. A handle.

Today after driving the wife to work I went to the donut shop at Supercentre. On the TV a guy was raking leaves and then they showed arrows like a weather map. It's amazing what they make a TV show out of now-a-days.

When I pulled out from the donut shop the morning guy on Rock 101 was doing Letterman's Top 10 list. That David Letterman's a funny guy, now I'm not saying he's not a funny guy, there was this one about people who slept, who slept at the White House. He said the big guy next to you on the plane is the president. I didn't quite catch all of that.

I got a coffee and an apple turnover. The air was smokey and I added to it, puffing away under the clicking air cleaner. The sugar crystals on the turnover were big, like road salt. I sat there and said shit, raised my hand to my mouth. It felt cold and sticky. I'd meant to wash the truck.

After I went and did that, I had to get out and check the plate. It'd come off the bolt and I hauled my screwdriver out of the glovebox and put it back on again.

» » »

When he got home he was going to make up a country tape for his cousin. His cousin and her current boyfriend'd got a spot in the Lion's place for people on low incomes. He had a record put out by the Nashville country music people in the fifties. It came with a book that had all their pictures in it. They were all on the cover too, a grid of guys with trucker's pompadours, short around the ears and square, thick jaws.

He jerked off quickly, had a shower, and made some

coffee while waiting for *The Simpsons* to come on at 10:00. *Remington Steele* was on at 11 and then *Perry Mason*. A commercial was on for the bartending school in Seattle. The guy was pulling out a strip of duct tape. He knew what he was saying even though the sound was killed. But he already had his bartending ticket.

The last job he had was working for three Japanese people who owned an Italian restaurant downtown. He wasn't racist. One of them owned another restaurant, the Japanese one down there. His wife was the other one plus a lady who had a kid. He liked it when this one lady was around because she was really sarcastic and ironic, totally acting like one of those old movies. »

«CHECK»

ALL DAY LONG the birds play in the back yard while you're at work. I think my cheque got here, but I don't feel like going around to the front of the house to see. It's 10:30. Your girlfriend called & she quit her job. Asked me if I was up yet. I said of course. She'd already been down at the UIC office.

What happened was this. When she brought the human rights case against him she had to go to this hearing. He got someone he'd worked with before to come in. He used to have people he worked with come to his bedroom where his studio was. Once this other woman was working on a project with him. She told the hearing she was in a neck brace from a car accident and had to lie on the floor in his studio for six weeks and he never touched her. He just said "cunt" "chick" "whore" "slut" except not just at his ex-girlfriends. And then he told this woman he called from her phone he was getting a blowjob from her in her office.

Now at the UIC they have you rub your fingertips on a TV screen. The white aluminum grills on either side reminded me of the grill on a classic car my dad took me to see at the exhibition building when I was 16. At the office this old poet was there, he had a big nose and a tweed jacket, once I saw him at some movie, I think it was *The Godfather*, but we didn't really chat much. There are pink blossoms everywhere and you can make enough just waitressing. »

«SMOKING HOLE»

SHE WAS A BABE, total fox, wore these cunt-cutters, Big Blue or US Tops, shaped jeans with no back pockets that hugged her labia like a swollen capital W. Geoffie had the usual junior high drug dealers Mars Bar-brown 3/4 length coat, belt left by his coke-head uncle in London, Ontario. He had a moustache and sometimes a bit of a beard, hair he washed once a week, curled up among circular cousins of same on his coat shoulders. His nut-hugger bellbottoms were almost femme in the way they palmed smooth his hips. She always managed to have a full mickey in her purse and a bottle of Coppertone baking butter in her pocket. She'd pinch her nipples for 45 seconds a time in the girls' room.

He'd roll one up before they headed for the smoke pit like anyone else in grade 9 doing their 12 times table. 12, 24, 36, 48, uh, 60, 72, 84, 96, um 118, now it was tricky, 132, 144 not what you'd expect. Put the rest of the Players back into the deck, half the tobacco from one in the fattie.

And so when Paco spat those miniature green garbage bags of crack into his hand—peas in a farmer's son's furrowed hand—thinking Geoffie'd asked for "up" not "skunk," and G'd already forked over the 15 bucks, the cazh way the El Salvadoran dealer handed back the money and recommended Pigeon Square, not Victory Park, for what you want bud, trying to squeeze a drop of blood from a sugar cube, showed how they're entrepreneurs as stoic as donut shop owners in small town Ontario beset with bikers and garrulous bladder busters, asscheeks floursacking over stools. How they could ignore the turf war, as dangerous as that between carpet remnant dealers or suburban strip-mall superstore lighting stores, with the resources of brothers and minor trailer park mafioso to call upon, the turf war where a man shot another man in the face, the defaced unlucky one unluckily'll never be deported for the third time now. The authorities don't deport corpses, faceless or no.

The bar Geoffie chose was quiet and clean and empty and smelled of bleach. A mural on the wall showed 3 longhouses in Bella Coola, one with the name of the bar's hotel, and there was a commuter bridge in the background, pretty like a wedding cake. *Ricki Lake* was half over. The show was about women who wanted their sons to go back to their own kid's mother, not the slut they were with now. Everyone was pretty excited. Some of them tho, it was hard to say why, he couldn't tell exactly what'd happened. 2 or 3 commercials for the show came on, then some real commercials, then some more commercials for the show, then the show again. People were just getting pissed off but he couldn't follow it, it was getting too loud in the bar.

» » »

When Geoffie got home that night the neighbour Frank was on his porch with two dogs playing and barking.

So Geoff, you see the sun today?

No. Maybe once.

Yep. It's . . . she's sure something. That rain. And if

it snows tonite that stretch down south, she won't stand the strain.

I know. So you got 2 dogs now?

No, this one, the pup's from across the street.

Oh right.

He's going eh?

Pretty bouncey for a pup.

You're telling me. Only 4 months. Just had 'im fixed.

Oh yeah?

Yeah, guess they use lasers to stitch them up now eh?

Really?

Yeah, and hasn't slowed him down much.

No he's going.

Yeah, 'cause she was looking at him today, you know her across the way eh, and she couldn't find the stitches, so she called 'em up.

. . . oh.

Yeah and so that's what they told them.

Oh yeah. Still wouldn't want to have it done though.

No. Me neither. »

«THE JESUS SEX DOLL BOX»

I LIKE THAT BELL they got, you know. The tarnished brass smell as it tinkles in the doorway. I come in and stamp my feet on that rubber there, there's slush on them. My pants're tucked into zip-up rubber boots the Air Force gives you. I've got the box with the Jesus Sex Doll folded back up inside it under my arm. On the stereo they've got—a chick is on, saying her daddy up and left her. The girl there came up from behind the counter. She's got a coffee from the place down the street and her girlfriend's sitting on the bench by the cash. I know the girlfriend, she goes to the mall with my daughter. The girl on cash says, yeah sure I'll get Sharona to babysit for me. Her eyes get a bit big when

I heave the sex doll Jesus container onto the counter.

Hi I say. I want to return this, it's defective.

Oh no she says brushing back a bang.

She phones her boss down island. She can't quite believe it. Apparently she has to check it to see if it's been used. She asks the girlfriend on the bench to watch the store while she goes down the street to get some surgical gloves.

She gets back and it's been quiet in the store, there isn't any music on the stereo anymore and you can hear a tow truck or snowplow or skateboarder crunch by.

She pulls the gloves out of the drugstore bag, they're more transparent than the bag and paler than her skin. She puts them on and looks like a doctor or veterinarian or hairdresser. She has eagles on her top. She puts a hand up Jesus's vagina and grimaces as her fingers scoop up some of my semen.

She checks the other two orifices and then strips off the gloves, folding them up into themselves. She gets out a utility knife and starts to behead Jesus. Hey, I say, surprised. What the fuck're you doin'?

It's store policy she says, grunting with the effort. The PVC is kind of resistant, for all its seam-popping possibilities.

Gotta send it back for credit. They don't want the whole thing.

Oh well Jesus, I say. That's . . . and I ponder on it for a spell. Finally I say no, don't, stop.

Too late. She pulls the knife back with a poultry deboning motion and takes Jesus's head off his body and sets it next to the candy jar of flavoured condoms. The girlfriend on the bench laughs and says, hey look at this, and puts a chocolate condom into Jesus's mouth.

Later, I drove home with Jesus sitting next to me. We duct-taped his head back on after I said I wanted to keep the sex doll after all.

That condom didn't taste too good in my mouth man, Jesus said.

Yeah. Sorry 'bout that.

Took your own sweet time too, didn't you? But thanks for taking back all of me. I know you would've been happy with just the head.

Yeah, well. »

Clint Burnham was born in Comox, B.C. in 1962. He has lived in France, Germany, Arvida, Bagotville, Edmonton, Goose Bay, Cold Lake, Regina, Victoria, Toronto, and Vancouver. He is the author of *The Jamesonian Unconscious: The Aesthetics of Marxist Theory; Fatal femmes: the poetry of Lynn Crosbie;* a collection of poetry, *Be Labour Reading* and numerous chapbooks. A new volume of poetry, *Buddyland*, is forthcoming from Coach House Books. Clint has served on the editorial collective of *Fuse* magazine, and was a contributing editor for *Paragraph* and *Boo*.

» » »